"Denton? What are you doing here?"

"I'm escorting you to the debate."

Her eyes narrowed. "Escorting me to the debate?"

"That's right. In light of the recent threats against you, your father has hired me as your bodyguard. He didn't mention it?"

Her eyes narrowed further. "No, he did not. I'd say I don't need a bodyguard, but I think we'd both know I was lying if I did."

Good, she knew the reality of the situation. That made his job somewhat easier.

Senator Philips strode into the room. "Denton! Thanks for coming out at such short notice. I begged Elle to take a long vacation somewhere until all of this passed, but she refused."

"There's a chance she wouldn't be safe on vacation, either, Senator. We still need to figure out who we're dealing with here, but my gut feeling is that these guys aren't going to let anything stop them."

Elle shivered, her cool confidence leaving her gaze a moment, replaced with fear.

Books by Christy Barritt

Love Inspired Suspense

Keeping Guard
The Last Target
Race Against Time
Ricochet
*Key Witness

*The Security Experts

CHRISTY BARRITT

loves stories and has been writing them for as long as she can remember. She gets her best ideas when she's supposed to be paying attention to something else—like in a workshop or while driving down the road.

The second book in her Squeaky Clean Mystery series, *Suspicious Minds,* won the inspirational category of the 2009 Daphne du Maurier Award for Excellence in Suspense and Mystery. She's also the coauthor of *Changed: True Stories of Finding God in Christian Music.*

When she's not working on books, Christy writes articles for various publications. She's also a weekly feature writer for the *Virginian-Pilot* newspaper, the worship leader at her church and a frequent speaker at various writers' groups, women's luncheons and church events.

She's married to Scott, a teacher and funny man extraordinaire. They have two sons, two dogs and a houseplant named Martha.

To learn more about her, visit her website, www.christybarritt.com.

KEY
WITNESS

Christy Barritt

Love Inspired

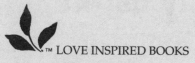 ™ LOVE INSPIRED BOOKS

ISBN-13: 978-0-373-44527-1

KEY WITNESS

Copyright © 2013 by Christy Barritt

www.LoveInspiredBooks.com

Printed in U.S.A.

Wherever you set foot, you will be on land I have given you.... No one will be able to stand against you as long as you live. For I will be with you as I was with Moses. I will not fail you or abandon you.
—*Joshua* 1:3–9

This book is dedicated to all of the wonderful people who've believed in me and pushed me to follow my dreams throughout the years. Your encouragement hasn't gone unnoticed or unappreciated.

A special thanks goes out to the brave, brilliant and inspiring gang over at the Norfolk FBI Field Office. Thanks for giving me a glimpse into your world and patiently answering my questions.

ONE

"Everyone down! Any quick moves and we'll shoot. Understand?"

Elle Philips dropped onto the marble floor of the bank. The contents of her purse scattered everywhere as she hit the ground, but she didn't care. She remained frozen, not wanting to draw attention to herself.

At the sound of approaching footsteps, her heart rate quickened. She raised her head, just enough to take a quick inventory of the situation. Two men. Black masks. Guns.

Elle knew that only two tellers were working right now, and that the manager had just left for a late lunch—Elle had passed him on her way in. Three other customers had also sunk to the floor. A frail-looking older woman, a college-aged girl and Denton. The dark-haired man had been in line behind her today. She knew Denton's name, only because they often came to the bank on the same days, same times. Over the weeks, they'd been flirtatious as they passed time in line.

Today, they'd only begun their casual teasing of each other when the robbers had burst through the doors of StoneCrest Bank on General Booth Blvd. in Virginia Beach, Virginia. At the moment, Elle glanced at Denton. He sat only a few feet away. His perceptive eyes met hers, silently communicating the urgency of the situation. Something about his calm gaze made her racing heart slow for a moment.

The shorter of the two robbers locked the glass doors at the front of the bank. He then stepped between the customers, the barrel of his gun bouncing against his black pants. The second robber, the one who'd ordered everyone to the ground, rushed toward the tellers, a bag in hand. "If you do what we say, no one will get hurt."

The first robber—Shortie, Elle nicknamed him—kicked Elle's purse back to her, sending more lipstick and pens rolling everywhere. "Give me your cell phones. If anyone even tries to call the police, I'll...I'll kill you."

A shudder ripped down Elle's spine, and her hands trembled as she riffled through her purse. Most of the contents lay askew, but her cell phone remained lodged in one of the deep pockets, refusing to budge. The device seemed to hang on tighter as Shortie loomed over her.

"Come on, lady!"

Finally, she jerked the phone from its hideout. Its metal burned in her hands, reminding her that this was her lifeline to the outside world. If only she could call the police...

No, let them get their money and get out of here, she told herself. Be compliant. That's what security experts always said. If only she weren't so bad at embracing compliance. Still, she was levelheaded enough to know when to back off.

She shoved her phone into Shortie's gloved hand. He grunted as he snatched it from her. Once all the phones were collected in a black bag, the man laid them on the counter at the center of the bank.

Julie, the young teller behind the counter, raised her hands in the air. Her eyes stretched wide with fear. "Whatever you want. Just don't hurt anyone."

The other robber, the ringleader, Elle thought, shoved his

gun at the teller. "I want all of the money in your drawer. If the police show up right now, you'll be the first one I take out."

Just do what they say, Elle prayed. Then maybe they would leave. The police could come and get some fingerprints and take eyewitness accounts. The justice system would be the heroes when they tracked down the robbers. Elle prayed that no one would try to be heroic and end up making the situation worse for all of them.

"What are you doing?" Ringleader shouted at Julie.

Elle wanted nothing more than to lay a steady hand on the young woman's shoulder and encourage her to just do what the man said. Instead, Elle hunkered down on the cool floor, her back against the wall. The best thing she could do would be to remain quiet and unseen.

Shortie paced over to her, his job obviously to guard the customers as Ringleader grabbed the money.

Elle tried to remember each detail so she could tell the police when they arrived. She soaked in the robbers' demeanors, their clipped words, the color of their eyes. As a campaign manager for her father's senate reelection bid, she was paid to pay attention to details. Shortie's gaze darted toward Elle, and she sucked in a breath, waiting to see what he would do.

Don't make this any worse than it has to be, buddy.

He waved his gun at her, and Elle noticed his hand trembling. The man was a novice at this. Was that a good or bad thing? The other man, Ringleader, didn't seem nervous at all.

"I need more money than that. Open the other drawers!" Ringleader leaned toward Julie, his gun aimed at her temple.

Julie shook her head, tears glimmering in her eyes. "I can't. I don't have their keys!"

"What do you mean, you don't have their keys? Can't you get them?"

"Only the branch manager has access to all the keys. You

have to have them to open the drawers." Tears glistened in her eyes.

"You're messing with me! Just get the keys, give me the money and nobody gets hurt."

Denton's strong, steady voice broke through the mayhem. "Can I see if I can help her?"

Shortie pointed his gun at him. "You know something about banks?"

Denton raised his hands. "No, but I want to help. You're making her nervous. Maybe I can help her open the drawer."

The gun trembled in Shortie's hands. "I want you to stay right where you are."

"I just don't want anyone to get hurt." Denton's gaze remained level and even.

Elle had to admire Denton's calm demeanor. She glanced at him again, at the chisel of his features, at the dark hair that formed the shadow of a beard across his face. Dark, thick hair. Tall, broad form. Put it all together, and he was the picture-perfect definition of a heartbreaker.

Elle noted that Denton wasn't wearing his customary suit and tie today. Instead, he'd donned a black jacket over a T-shirt and jeans. In all of their casual conversation, Elle had never thought to ask him what he did for a living. Perhaps he was in law enforcement of some sort? How else could he be so calm in this situation?

Ringleader pointed his gun at the other teller. "Put your money in now!" The teller filled his bag, but then he turned his attention back to Julie. "Figure out how I can get more money." He reached over and grabbed Elle's arm, pulling her to her feet. The gun went to her head. "Do it now or she dies."

Elle gasped and trembles overtook her.

"Calm down," Denton said. He still leaned against the wall, his knees propped up, his voice and movement as calm and controlled as if he were merely talking everyone else through a training exercise. "Let her go."

Ringleader paced over to him, Elle in tow. "Are you in charge here? I didn't think so. You're going to be next if you don't keep your mouth shut."

Elle's throat burned. She was acutely aware of the gun at her temple. One accidental jerk of the finger and she'd be dead, just like that.

There was so much she still wanted to do, needed to do. Life came into an odd and complete clarity when the end appeared close enough to touch. Her necklace, the one her grandmother gave her before she passed, seemed to sear into her skin at the moment. It reminded her that she'd made a promise to her grandmother that she still needed to fulfill.

"I'm telling you—I can't get into the other drawers or the vault. They're all locked, and I don't have the keys. The manager's out to lunch." Sweat glistened across Julie's forehead.

Something hard hit Elle in the face. She blanched before sinking to her knees. The robber quickly pulled her right back up. Her legs would hardly hold her. It didn't matter. Ringleader held her up by her coat collar.

Her cheek throbbed from where the man had pistol-whipped her. Tears rushed to her eyes as pain continued to send shocks through her.

"That's only the start of what's going to happen if you don't get me more money." The man's hot breath hit her cheek, along with a splattering of spittle.

"Boss, you said no one would get hurt," Shortie said.

"I've got this. You shut your mouth and keep the crowd under control."

"Let me—let me…let me search my manager's desk, see if I can find any keys," the second teller said.

Ringleader pushed Elle back to the ground. She stumbled

until she hit the wall and sank to the floor. Her hand went to her cheek, and she felt moisture there. Blood? Tears? Both?

Denton looked over at her, his eyes full of concern. "Are you okay?" he mouthed.

She nodded, grateful to be alive. But how much longer would that be the case? The robbers were obviously losing it, getting out of control. This whole situation could spiral into something much bigger than even they had planned.

"Thank you," she whispered back.

The men were pacing now, as if trying to figure out what to do next.

"Good gravy, you didn't know the manager was gone for lunch?" Ringleader let out an expletive and stared at his partner in crime.

"He usually goes earlier."

"Usually isn't good enough." He turned back to Julie. "You need to figure out a plan B."

"Me? Me? How am I supposed to figure out a plan B?" Panic claimed her voice, her limbs.

"You have to know another way to get into that vault."

Julie's head swung back and forth. "Not without a key and a code."

Ringleader cocked the gun at her. "Think a little harder."

She half moaned, half screamed. "I've been trying. I have. There's nothing I can do!"

The gun fired. Elle screamed as Julie disappeared from sight, sinking below the counter.

Denton jumped to his feet. Elle slapped her hand over her mouth, disbelief filling her.

Julie. The robber had just shot Julie.

She lifted a prayer as tears rushed to her eyes. The seriousness of the situation hit her at full force. This was bad. Really bad.

"Stay down!" Ringleader swung around, his gun aimed

at the crowd, as if telling them that any one of them could be next.

Elle's gaze flew to the potted plant beside her. She'd seen something fly from the man's belt when he swung around. Her eyes widened when she spotted a cell phone there. Had the robber's cell phone really just flown off his belt and into the plant?

Elle glanced back up at him. He didn't seem to notice the device had slipped off. If she reached her hand out just a little, she could grab it.

But if he caught her, what would he do? Slap her again? Something worse? The thought of Julie flashed through her mind.

She glanced over and saw Denton staring at her. He'd obviously noticed the phone also. What was he trying to tell her? To forget about it? To grab it? What was the right thing to do? She wrestled with her choice. Flexed her fingers. Glanced back up at the robbers. They all seemed distracted by the second teller fumbling through her boss's desk.

This was Elle's chance.

She willed herself to move quickly and without notice, for her motions to be as fluid as flowing water. Before she could second-guess herself, she extended her hand. She grabbed the phone and slipped it into her coat pocket.

Her gaze darted around the room. No one appeared to see her…except Denton. His furrowed eyebrows showed his apprehension.

At least she'd now have some proof of who these men were. Maybe it would help the police put them behind bars.

Elle reached into her pocket and opened the phone. She held her breath, afraid of making any noise or drawing attention to what she was doing. Her heart rate slowed a moment when no one seemed to notice her. She felt the buttons until she found 9–1–1. She prayed the man wouldn't notice his phone was gone, that he wouldn't realize Elle had taken it.

"Any of you want to be next?" Ringleader's voice didn't rise in pitch. He sounded so detached at the moment that Elle felt a chill race through her.

"She's dead. Is she dead? Did you kill her?" Shortie's voice, on the other hand, rose in panic. "What are you doing?"

"They're going to pay!"

As the minutes stretched on, Elle watched the two men pace and listened to them mutter. Every second Julie was without medical care put the woman more at risk. Elle wished more than anything she could go check on the teller, that she could give the robbers the money so they'd be gone.

The phone burned in her pocket.

Had the dispatcher heard what was going on? Had they sent help?

Elle prayed that the answer was yes.

Shortie looked at the front door. "Do you hear that? Sirens. We've got to run before they get here, man! The police are right around the corner."

Ringleader grabbed his bag of cash and darted to the door.

Elle breathed a sigh of relief. He hadn't noticed his cell phone. No one else had been hurt.

Just as the robbers stepped out the front door, the Ringleader reached for his waistline. Felt the empty space where his phone was. Then he looked up. Looked at Elle. He knew she had his phone. She'd been closest to him. Certainly, her gaze held telltale guilt. The robber's eyes narrowed before he pulled his finger across his throat.

Elle sucked in a breath. He was going to find her. And when he did, he would kill her.

Mark Denton saw the robber make the throat-slitting motion as he ran from the bank.

He looked over at the raven-haired beauty and saw that her face had gone ghost-white.

What Elle had done had been incredibly risky, but she may have just saved all of their lives—at least the life of the bank teller.

With the men gone, Denton jumped from the floor and propelled himself over the counter. The bank teller had been shot in the stomach. Blood stained her shirt. Denton took off his jacket and placed it over the wound to stop the bleeding.

"Someone wave the ambulance inside. She needs help. Now!"

Elle rushed to the door. She paused momentarily at it, as if she were afraid the robbers might be waiting on the other side for her. But she stepped outside anyway.

Denton already admired her spunk and guts. Not everyone would have handled themselves so well in a situation like this. Denton, a former SEAL, now worked special operations for a Department of Defense contractor, and even he'd been thrown off-kilter some. He knew moves that could have taken down the robbers, but there were two of them and they had guns. Plus, there were too many people who could have been casualties if something went wrong. He'd taken the restrained approach. He hoped it had been the right one.

"It's going to be okay," he told the teller. Her eyes drifted shut, as if she were losing consciousness. He had to keep her lucid until the paramedics got in here.

"They're on their way!" Elle shouted from the door. "Over here!"

A moment later, two EMTs came into view, pulling a stretcher behind them. Elle closed her eyes, as if praying. This teller was going to need some prayers, not just to recover from the physical wounds but to overcome the emotional impact of what had just happened to her, too. He lifted up a prayer, as well.

As soon as the EMTs took over, Denton stood, his hands and undershirt now covered with blood. But he was alive. As of right now, they were all alive. The police began swarming the place and soon Denton would have to give his account of the incident. For now he was satisfied to know that everyone else was okay.

Elle approached him, taking in the sight of his blood-stained hands. "Are you all right?"

"I'm fine. That was a gutsy move on your part, though."

"I saw an opportunity and had to take it." She shoved her hands into her coat and pulled out the phone.

He reached for it. "Do you mind?"

"Not at all."

Denton opened the phone, anxious to see if the robbers had any personal identification on the device. He scrolled through the menu, but saw no names or phone numbers saved.

"Probably untraceable."

Elle nodded and pulled a hair behind her ear. "I figured as much."

Suddenly, the phone buzzed in his hand. Elle's eyes met his. "Is someone calling?"

Denton noted the Unknown Caller on the screen before flipping the phone open. "Looks like a text message."

Elle leaned over his shoulder. "What does it say?"

Denton's throat felt dry as he read the words. He glanced up at Elle, trying to soften the message. It was no use. "It says, 'I'll find you and kill you.'"

TWO

Elle held a cold compress to her cheek and leaned back into the padded leather chair at the police station. All of the witnesses from the bank had been questioned separately, and Elle had poured out everything she could remember. Right now, her cheek and head throbbed, and she desperately wanted to go home, take a long bath and fall asleep.

Sleep. She wanted a restful sleep, but knew she'd have nightmares for a long time about what had happened. The violence she'd seen today was so out of the realm of her upright—perhaps uptight—little world.

One of the officers went to get her some water, so she stood and stretched for a moment. Were the other witnesses still here? Suddenly, the room she was in felt too small and suffocating.

She stepped into the hallway and heard Denton's voice in the distance. She followed the sound, for some reason finding comfort in the man's presence. She crept down the hallway until she reached another office, this one with the door open. Denton sat across from a detective, leaning back in his chair as if exhausted. His voice still sounded steady and strong, though, as it drifted into the hallway.

"One of the men was definitely more dominant. If I had to guess based on his speech pattern, he's from the Northwest and most likely a blue-collar worker. He had a slight limp and, from the way he carried himself, I'd say he was in his mid- to late-twenties." Denton spotted Elle and straightened. "Hey there."

She stepped into the office, lowering the compress to get a better look at Denton. "You picked up on all of that?"

He shrugged, a hint of cockiness in the action. "I'm good at being observant."

"I thought I was, too, but I didn't notice half of that."

The phone rang and the detective across the desk held up a finger as if to say "wait." Elle leaned in the doorway, watching the detective's expression change from serious to disgusted. She braced herself as he hung up and turned to them. "That was the officer I sent to the hospital. He told me that the teller just passed away. This investigation has just moved from armed robbery to homicide."

Elle's heart sank. She'd hoped the EMTs had arrived in time and that everything would be okay. She sank into the chair beside Denton, suddenly light-headed.

"She was saving to go to college, you know." Julie's bright, smiling face stained her memory. "She wanted to be a teacher."

Denton raised an eyebrow. "She told you that? Were you friends?"

Elle shrugged. "I've been going into that bank every week for the past three years. You start to feel like you know each other. Her life was worth so much more than the money those men got away with."

"Three thousand dollars is what the bank manager calculated," the detective said. "You can't put a price on a life. The K-9s are trying to follow the robbers' scent now. We're also checking all of the surveillance video from around the area. We're going to get the sketches and description of the men out to the media in time for the evening news, we hope. Between all of those things, I'm hopeful that we'll get these guys."

Denton shifted in his seat. "I'm not so sure you're going to catch them." He shook his head, his eyes narrowed. "I don't know. Something about the entire setup is bugging me. I mean, Julie cooperated with them. She gave them all the money she could, but they still shot her. That doesn't make sense to me. Why would they shoot her? The dominant robber didn't even hesitate."

"What are you getting at?" the detective asked.

"It was almost like they went into the bank with the intention of killing someone." Denton shook his head. "It sounds terrible, but that's what my gut is telling me."

An officer stepped into the room, his gaze focused on Elle. "Ms. Philips, your father is here to see you. I told him you were almost done, but he insisted on seeing you right away."

Before Elle could even stand, her father rushed into the room. Two of his men shadowed him, remaining right outside the door. "Elle, sweetheart, are you okay? I was so worried when I heard what happened."

She nodded and fell into his arms. "I'm fine, Dad. Just a few cuts and bruises." She stepped back. "Dad, this is Denton—"

"Mark Denton," her father interrupted, a grin stretched across his face. He extended his hand and pumped it up and down. "Good to see you again."

"Senator Philips."

Elle looked back and forth between them. "You know each other?"

Her father placed his hand on Denton's shoulder. "Denton has worked security detail for me in the past."

Elle's gaze fixated on Denton. She realized there was so much she didn't know about the man. "Security detail?"

A hint of a smile curled Denton's lips. "I'm a private security contractor."

Elle nodded as the truth seemed to settle over her. "No wonder you handled yourself so well during the robbery."

Her father turned to her and nodded slowly—what Elle called his "thoughtful politician nod." The senator added, "He's the best, of course, because I only hire the best."

Denton rubbed his five o'clock shadow before resting his hands on his hips. "Your daughter called 9–1–1 when one of the robbers dropped his phone. The operator heard what was going on in the background and put a trace on the phone. The police were just two blocks away when dispatch called them. I think we're lucky that only one life was lost today."

"That's my girl. She thinks quickly on her feet, just like I raised her. She didn't graduate at the top of her class from Yale because of luck." Her dad's eyes shone with pride.

Elle had to tell her father the rest of the story. "But Dad—"

"I know. The robber threatened you. He seemed to put it together that you were the one who found his phone. The detective filled me in when he called me."

The detective called him? Of course he had. Her father had connections all throughout the state—the country, for that matter. An incident involving a senator's daughter wouldn't be taken lightly. "I was the only one close by in the area where he'd been standing. He must have put it together."

"I'm used to getting threats. I don't like it when my little girl gets them, though." Elle could see the concern in her father's eyes. But just hearing him call her "little" in public tore at the image she'd tried to build of herself as a self-sufficient career woman.

"I'm not little anymore, Daddy."

Her father grinned. "You'll always be little to me, no matter how old you are."

Denton shoved his hands down into his pockets. "The good

news is that these robbers can't be the brightest bulbs in the socket. One of them did leave his cell phone at the scene of the crime. That alone should merit an article in the 'Stupid Criminal' section of the news."

Elle sucked in a deep breath at the mention of an article. How could she have forgotten?

"What is it?" Denton leaned toward her.

She licked her lips, her gaze meeting her father's. "There's an article about me running in tomorrow's paper. It's a feature piece about my life and my work with my dad." She swallowed, her throat suddenly dry. "If the robbers didn't know who I was today, they're going to find out soon."

Denton had seen Elle's face go from pale to even paler throughout the course of the day. But as she remembered the article, her face went stark white. The article would apparently put everything out there about her and, if the robbers saw it, they'd have all they needed to track her down.

"You can stay with us tonight." His father hooked his arm around her neck. "I'm sure they'll catch these guys soon. You just lay low until then."

"Can you call the paper and see if they can pull it?" Denton asked.

"I can try, but it's late. The paper has probably already gone to press."

"How big of an article is it?"

Elle shrugged. "I'm not sure. Hopefully it will be buried on the last page, right? After all, I'm not that interesting. What could they possible say about me?"

Denton was sure a reporter could find a lot to say about the daughter of a prominent senator who was up for reelection. Elle didn't seem like the naive type, though. Certainly she realized that, also.

She extended her hand. "Denton, I wish I could say it was a pleasure to meet you, but under the circumstances…"

He grasped her hand, surprised at her skin's softness. "I understand."

Her father ushered her away. As soon as she was gone, Denton missed her. The woman had intelligent eyes, a courageous spirit and drop-dead gorgeous looks—petite and trim with an olive complexion, long, dark hair with just a touch of curl, and warm brown eyes. It wasn't that he was looking for a relationship. No, he wasn't ready for another one of those yet. But the woman was a nice distraction from the rather grueling hours he'd spent staring evil in the face.

Right now, as she left, Denton had the urge to go with her, to be that extra set of eyes in case the robbers—killers, now—somehow tracked her down. But he didn't know the woman well enough to simply tag along. Besides, her dad was a senator. He could afford protection if she needed it.

An officer was waiting to take him back to his SUV, still parked in the lot at the bank. He needed to drive back to the Iron, Inc. headquarters. The organization, also known as Eyes, was an elite paramilitary security firm. They only hired the best—former special operations officers, FBI and CIA agents and other heroes of law enforcement. Denton was holding down the fort, so to speak, while his boss, Jack Sergeant, was on his honeymoon.

Every time he thought of Jack's marriage, his heart panged with both joy for his friend and sadness for himself. How long had it been now since Wendi passed away? Two years? Sometimes it felt like decades, and other moments it seemed like just yesterday.

They'd been married only for three years when she was diagnosed with a brain tumor. She died two years later. They'd enjoyed every moment they had, holding on to the hope that they'd grow old and gray together. That dream didn't happen, though.

No one had caught his eye since Wendi. So why couldn't he get Elle out of his mind? What was it about the woman that intrigued him so much? The last thing he wanted was a relationship. He still hadn't gotten over the heartbreak of losing Wendi, and sometimes he doubted he ever would.

His mind drifted to that article that Elle had mentioned. What unfortunate timing.

Buried. Yes, he hoped that article would be buried among others, and that the robbers didn't bother reading the newspaper. Hopefully they could simply move on from this tragedy today, and Elle would piece back together her life as it was before she watched someone she knew get fatally wounded in front of her.

He prayed today would be the end of this nightmare. So why did he have the feeling it wasn't?

Elle hadn't even made it down the steps and to the breakfast table when her dad stopped her and held up the newspaper. There on the front page was a picture of Elle, smiling with her feet propped up on her desk and her dad's picture on the table behind her.

So much for the story getting buried.

"Lovely picture, darling." Her father kissed her cheek, but his eyes still wore a scowl. "This is great publicity careerwise, but terrible publicity in light of what happened yesterday."

"Did they misquote me again?"

"If they did, they only made you sound better, if that's possible. In fact, they made you sound quite genius. I only wish the article hadn't come out now. I'm really quite worried."

She took the paper and began reading as she walked to the kitchen for her first cup of coffee. The article profiled her work for her father as campaign manager, calling her the "brains" behind his reelection campaign. It highlighted her educational accomplishments, as well as her reign as Miss Virginia. Each of the carefully plotted-out details of her life, all which had run a smooth course thus far.

Too bad she was becoming more and more restless with each passing day. She wanted more than anything to help with her father's reelection campaign, but a career in politics was something she was ready to put behind her.

Elle folded the paper as her mother—who already looked picture-perfect with her dark, chin-length hair carefully styled, her makeup applied and her business-casual outfit crisp—hurried into the room with a touch-pad computer in hand.

She squeezed Elle's shoulder before sitting across from her. "Morning, darling."

"Morning, Mother."

She placed the computer on the table and an electronic version of Elle's article stared up at them. "Nice article, dear. I've already gotten several emails about it. Bob Allen, eat your heart out if you think you're going to win this election."

"Bob Allen is behind in the polls by eight percent. There's no way he'll beat us."

Her mother winked at her. "That's the spirit." She leaned toward her and squinted. "That's a nasty bump on your cheek. You tried any concealer?"

"Not yet."

"Be sure before your father's debate tonight, okay?"

The debate tonight. Elle had almost forgotten. Images of Julie at the bank yesterday had squeezed out any other thoughts. How could life go on after a tragedy like that? How could her family talk as if nothing had happened?

She already knew the answer to that. If it didn't involve politics, it didn't involve her family.

Though her parents loved her, Elle was certain that their first thought after what happened yesterday, right after her safety, was "How can we spin this to our advantage?" Such was the nature of politics.

Elle finished breakfast and retreated to the sunroom. Work was the best distraction for her at the moment. She pulled up the email on her laptop, leaned back into the cushy wicker chair and took a sip of coffee.

Before she could get too involved with her work, her mind drifted to Denton. She'd enjoyed chatting with him every week at the bank. It was too bad that those memories would forever be scarred. But maybe it was better that way. Denton seemed like just the kind of man she could fall for—only he was the type that she *shouldn't* fall for. The type who'd only break her heart. She knew the personality of someone with his job description—they always lived for the next adventure, always looked forward to taking the next risk. She'd learned the hard way that men like that weren't the type to commit.

She sighed and began sorting through her messages, shooting off quick responses to several inquiries. Staying busy would be the best way to help her forget about what had happened yesterday.

The last message on her screen caught her eye. Spam, she assumed. That or someone from another country claiming they needed her help receiving a million-dollar inheritance.

She clicked on the message, ready to hit Delete when the words on the screen stopped her.

What do you think about dying a slow, painful death? Get used to the idea because it's your fate. The fun is only beginning, Elle Philips. Prepare yourself for the adventure ahead.

She screamed and dropped her coffee.

Denton stepped into Senator Philip's elaborate, stately study and saw Elle in the distance, dressed in a black business suit, clipboard in hand and talking animatedly to a group surrounding her. She didn't hear him enter the room, so he took a moment to observe.

She had a slender figure. Tiny chin, big eyes, flawless skin and silky brown hair that fell below her shoulders. Not that he'd noticed.

He'd always known she was beautiful—anyone could see that. But it was the genuine kindness in her eyes that set her apart from all the other pretty women out there. Some females in her position would be snotty or unapproachable. But Elle was grounded, and she had a smile that would set anyone at ease.

He cleared his throat. Her head swung toward him, and her eyes widened in surprise.

"Denton?" She excused herself and walked toward him. The knot on her face had been nicely concealed, and Denton could hardly tell anything had happened to her yesterday. "What are you doing here?"

"I'm escorting you to the debate."

Her eyes narrowed. "Escorting me to the debate?"

"That's right. In light of the recent threats against you, your father has hired me as your bodyguard. He didn't mention it?"

Her eyes narrowed further. "No, he did not. I'd say I don't need a bodyguard, but I think we'd both know I was lying if I did."

Good, she knew the reality of the situation. That made his job somewhat easier than working with someone in denial of the danger they faced. He had to admit that he'd been relieved when Senator Philips had called him this morning. Really, Denton should have assigned one of his men to this job so he could oversee operations at Eyes. But Denton knew he couldn't trust this one to anyone else. Besides, Senator Philips had requested him personally.

The senator strode into the room. "Denton! Thanks for

coming out at such short notice. I begged Elle to take a long vacation somewhere until all this passed, but she refused."

"There's a chance she wouldn't be safe on vacation, either, Senator. We still need to figure out who we're dealing with here, but my gut feeling is that these guys aren't going to let anything stop them."

Elle shivered, her cool confidence leaving her gaze a moment, replaced with fear. As quickly as it disappeared, her facade returned.

"I'm sorry to be so brutally honest, Elle, but you need to know who you're dealing with here. My team of profilers has been—"

Elle placed a hand on her hip, eyes wide in disbelief. "Your team of profilers? Who are you guys, the FBI?"

Denton smirked. "We're like the FBI, only better."

Elle raised an eyebrow. "A little cocky, aren't you?"

He shrugged. "I'm just telling the truth. We only hire the best."

"And why would people want to work for you over an official government agency?"

"We pay better, for starters."

Her father stepped forward. "He's telling the truth. They're the best. Former FBI, CIA, Secret Service, military special operations, you name it."

"Excuse me for speaking about you as if you're not here for a moment, but, Dad, you said yesterday that Denton has worked for you before. When was that? Why don't I remember?"

"You were down taking care of your grandmother for that month before she passed. Almost two years ago. Remember we had that lobbyist making threats against me after one of my votes in the senate? I hired Denton then."

Elle nodded slowly. "I see."

Her father looked at his watch. "I must be going now. Denton will be driving you there." He leaned forward to kiss his daughter on the cheek. "Be safe, now."

As soon as he exited the room, Elle's gaze fell on Denton. "Let me just gather my things." She paused. "I really want to say that all of this is unnecessary. But it's not, is it?"

Denton shook his head. "That man hardly flinched when he killed Julie yesterday. If he and his partner are after money and they now realize you're a senator's daughter, then my guess is that they're seeing an opportunity they don't want to pass up."

Fear stained her eyes. "An opportunity?"

He nodded, knowing his words would feel like a slap in the face to Elle. "An opportunity they'd kill for."

THREE

Denton saw Elle shiver as his words settled on her. He'd found that being direct was always the best tactic, especially in life-or-death situations. But he hated to see a woman frightened. He especially hated to see Elle frightened.

Elle seemed to brush off her chills as she grabbed a briefcase and leather jacket. "No need to dwell on that too long right now." She nodded toward the front door. "Let's go."

Denton placed a hand on her back as they walked outside into the early autumn day. "I'm driving."

"Bodyguard and chauffeur? So much for trying to live like a normal person."

"I aim to please."

The whiff of her flowery perfume drifted to him on the October breeze. He recognized the scent from their talks at the bank. It was just one thing he enjoyed about running into her each week. That, her smile and her subdued wit.

He directed her to his black SUV, opened the door and waited as she climbed inside before jogging around to the driver's side. They were the last of the entourage to leave. As he started down the driveway, Elle waved at a guard stationed by a gate at the front of their house.

"Pull over a minute."

Denton did as directed. She rolled down her window and

smiled at the guard, a man probably in his early fifties with an almost completely bald head. "Happy birthday, Jimmy."

"You remembered. You're one in a million, Ms. Philips." The guard grinned, obviously pleased at the attention. His grin faded, though. "Your father told me about everything that happened. You be careful, now."

"Don't worry. My father put the best on the job." She nodded toward Denton.

Jimmy glanced at him, and Denton raised his chin, glad his sunglasses concealed his examination of the man. He appeared affable enough and truly seemed to adore Elle, in an almost fatherly way. Right now, though, Denton had to be suspicious of everyone.

"Take care of her, sir. The world would be a sad place without her."

"I plan on doing just that."

They pulled away, traveling down a lone country road that led away from the senator's estate. Elle stared pensively out the window as they rolled along. "You know where you're going?"

"The Virginia Beach Convention Center. The last of the debates between your father and his political challenger. About five thousand people are expected to come for the event, which will be televised on two of the three major networks and broadcasted to viewers in Virginia."

The perfect opportunity if someone wanted to show themselves and make a statement, Denton thought. His only security detail was protecting Elle, he reminded himself. There were other law enforcement officers there in charge of providing security for the event itself. The fact that Senator Philips would be there meant amped-up security in general.

Senator Philips seemed nice enough, in a politician sort of way. He was warm, the kind of man you might want to kick back with for hot dogs and a baseball game. He was obviously affectionate toward his daughter. But Denton had always believed that charm could be deceptive and, for that reason, Denton remained cautious around the man. That charm had gotten Senator Philips elected, but it was his ability to manipulate situations that had kept him in office.

"It sounds like you've done your homework."

"Don't expect—or accept—anything less."

"Don't worry. I won't." Her grin softened her words a bit.

Denton glanced over at Elle. "So you're the campaign manager for your father."

"I am. You didn't know that when you befriended me at the bank?"

"I just thought you were intriguing. I never expected to be your bodyguard or realized that I'd worked with your father in the past. He kept his family private. I was surprised he even approved of someone doing an article about you." Some aspects of the senator's family life were public—and purposely so. But many details were still kept as limited as possible, especially where Elle was concerned.

"The article was my idea. My father has had some rumors floating around about him recently, rumors that make him seem less than likable. I wanted to bring some positive PR to his campaign and make him seem more like a family man."

"You mean instead of a womanizer?"

She blanched. "Yes. I thought if people could see the part of my father that I saw, maybe he could gain an even bigger lead in the polls. My father was actually against it, truth be known."

"It was a nice article." It confirmed most of what he'd already assumed about her. She was smart, talented, beautiful and accomplished. "You're a former Miss Virginia, huh? Can you do the beauty pageant wave for me?"

She smiled and humored him with a little wave. He liked

seeing the goofy side of her instead of the always poised woman that she liked to present herself as.

He chuckled. "That factoid did surprise me. I didn't see you as the beauty pageant type."

"I'm not. My parents encouraged me to do it. They said it would look nice on my résumé and give me good experience. And I agree. It accomplished those things."

He glanced in his rearview mirror, checking to see if anyone was tailing them. Nothing suspicious caught his eye, but he still needed to remain on guard. Always watching, observing, calculating what-ifs.

"Is everything okay?" Elle's facade cracked a moment as her worry showed through.

"Everything's fine. I just have to keep my eyes open."

"It could have been an idle threat."

"Could be."

"But it might not be."

"Exactly."

She sighed, her shoulders slacking ever so slightly. "Don't people have better things to do than to scare or harm others? It makes no sense to me."

"Don't try to understand evil. It's useless."

"You're right. I guess I shouldn't even try. It's just—why would someone steal money instead of simply working for it? Don't people have enough to worry about in their own lives rather than making other people miserable?"

"I'd venture to say that most criminals aren't psychopaths. These men most likely have a motive behind what they're doing, a reason they're using to justify their actions. It could be the money—maybe they feel entitled, think that they deserve more than they have—or they could be trying to make a statement of some sort."

"Make a statement, huh? What kind of statement would they be trying to make with threatening me?"

"That's what we're trying to figure out."

"You mentioned your team of profilers earlier, but I cut you off. What did your team conclude?"

"One of the subjects is the dominant personality and the other is submissive. The dominant's emotions were tightly under control, while the submissive was taken by surprise by the murder. But even though the second subject seemed in the dark, we believe the crime was well thought-out, the murder perhaps even preplanned."

"Impressive. And chilling."

"The police are working the case right now. They're looking at video feeds from everywhere around the area."

"Did the K-9 unit turn up anything?"

"No, they lost the scent at about a block away. The suspects probably jumped into a getaway car."

"Does that mean there are three? A driver also?"

"There's always that chance."

"This isn't good."

Denton shook his head, wishing he could comfort her. But he couldn't. "You're right. It's not. But I'm not going to let you out of my sight until these guys are arrested."

Elle stood backstage, her arms folded over her chest as she watched the debate from the sidelines. Her dad had answered every question with educated, reasoned responses, even combining some humor into the mix. He had this election in the bag…at least, she hoped.

These threats against her had her unnerved enough. Then throw Mark Denton into the mix and she felt even more uneasy. Not because she didn't trust Denton—the opposite, in fact. She felt more drawn to the man than to anyone in a long time. But there was no room in her life to play with the idea of romance.

Not only was she incredibly busy with the campaign, but

her last relationship had completely shattered her trust in men. When she and Denton had innocently flirted at the bank, that had been one thing. But now she was going to be forced to work with the man for…how long? Who knew?

The man was handsome—too handsome for his own good, probably. He had a rakish grin that Elle was sure women swooned over. Not Elle, of course. His build was solid and muscular, and he stood at least six feet tall, maybe taller, with brown eyes that could melt the coldest of hearts—except Elle's. The man was confident, charming and he didn't take himself too seriously. He knew how to work a room and how to handle himself in a tense situation. He'd proven that. And Elle had always been a sucker for men like that.

But she couldn't be now. Not anymore. Not since Preston had taken every piece of trust she had for men and shredded it like yesterday's paperwork. Men were not trustworthy, and she had no trust to give. End of story. The one thing she feared in life was failing and letting people down. When things had ended with Preston, she'd let herself down. The humiliation and shame she felt afterward had solidified her resolve to stay single—forever, if necessary.

Denton stood beside her, his gaze scanning the crowds just as he'd been doing since they'd arrived. The person who'd sent her that email wasn't here tonight…or was he?

She prayed that the police would figure out the men's identities and quickly so she could resume life and focus on other, more important things.

Her best friend, Brianna, shimmied up beside her and leaned close. "Who's your escort?"

"He's…no one. I'll explain later. Long story."

Brianna raised her eyebrows, her eyes twinkling. "I can't wait to hear."

"It's not like that."

"Then what's it like?"

"Someone's threatened me."

"If someone threatens me, will I be forced to have someone who looks like him follow my every move? If so, bring on the threats."

"Brianna!" Elle scolded. "This is serious."

The sparkle left her friend's eyes. "You're right. I'm sorry to make light of it. Are you going to be okay?"

"She's going to be fine." Elle looked up and saw Denton glance at Brianna, the corner of his mouth curled. Apparently he'd heard their conversation.

At least Brianna had the decency to blush a little.

Bentley Davis, her father's chief-of-staff, bustled toward them. "The debate's wrapping up. You ready for the reception afterward with our campaign donors?"

Elle nodded. "Of course. I confirmed the audio setup and the catering this morning. Everything's in place."

"Perfect. I left a few more pledge cards in the dressing room. Some people aren't comfortable leaving any of their information online. Makes more work for us, though."

"It's no problem. I'll have Brianna enter the information." Bentley was always so concerned with his to-do list that he often turned people away with his off-putting manner. Elle prayed she'd never get so wrapped up in her goals that she forgot about the people around her.

As the debate ended, Elle turned to Denton. "Let me grab my things. The reception is in one of the conference rooms down the hall."

He didn't miss a beat as he fell into step beside her. "I'm coming with you."

"I'd expect nothing less."

Denton stayed close as they wove between people toward the dressing room. She had to admit—she felt safe with him nearby and, even without knowing a lot about him, she already trusted his competence and skill.

Elle's conversation with Brianna fluttered through her mind. She glanced over at Denton. "By the way, I apologize for my assistant earlier. She's always been the one who speaks before she thinks."

"No apologies necessary. She's your assistant?"

"As of two months ago she became my assistant. Before that, she was simply my best friend."

"Your best friend now works for you? Sounds like an interesting dynamic."

"She and her husband just split, and she's having trouble making ends meet right now. I needed an assistant so I hired her. It seems like a win-win...for now, at least."

"I see." He paused for a second. "Tell me more about Bentley Davis."

Elle's gaze cut to him, but she didn't slow her steps. "Bentley? He's worked with my dad for years, ever since Dad was a judge. Why do you ask?"

"Until we know who's behind these threats, everyone is a suspect."

"Even Bentley? He's quite annoying sometimes, but truly harmless." She pushed into the dressing room and spotted the papers atop her soft-as-butter leather briefcase. "Besides, if he'd been one of the robbers, I think I would have recognized him. They were strangers, remember?"

"Remember that things aren't always as they seem, Elle. And there could be a third person involved, someone you never saw or heard. Everything that happened yesterday could have been a ruse for something bigger. There are a lot of unknowns right now."

"I have a hard time believing anything other than that my involvement in this whole thing is random. It's the only thing that makes sense."

"Let me decide that."

She flipped through the correspondence with one hand

while she grabbed her briefcase with the other hand and swung it over her shoulder.

"Anything good?"

"Any support of my father's campaign is good." She glanced up and smiled. "But yes, there are some pledges in here that look promising."

She paused when she got to a sealed envelope. Why hadn't Bentley opened this one? She slid her fingernail through the paper and pulled out a card. She sucked in a breath, noting that this wasn't their normal correspondence.

"What is it?" Denton's hand covered hers.

She dropped the papers from her hands. They scattered across the floor as Elle backed away.

"Elle?"

She pointed at the floor. "There are pictures of me. From this morning." Reading on her laptop inside the sunroom. Drinking coffee by the window. Sitting pensively on the porch.

Denton picked one up. "Pictures? How did someone get pictures?"

"There was a message, too, Denton, stuck on a sticky note."

"What did it say?"

Terror seemed to freeze her expression, make her unable to move. "It said that 'Agony awaits.'"

"Is it really necessary for me to leave right now? Can't I just make an appearance at the reception?"

Denton kept a firm grip on her arm as he led her toward a door at the back of the building. "More than necessary. You do understand that the person who's threatening you was— maybe still is—here tonight, don't you?"

She nodded, her eyes dazed. "I do, but..." She paused from her distress to shake hands with a few people who tried to chat with her about the debate. Denton urged her onward. Once she escaped from the crowd's grasp, she looked up at him. "I don't know what to think right now. This is just crazy."

"The police are going to search for any evidence here. They're sending me the security tapes so we can see who's been in and out of your dressing room. No one, other than authorized personnel, should have had access to that area, though. I want to know how someone got back there."

"You need to talk to Bentley."

"Oh, don't worry. I will. Just as soon as I know you're safe. Which, right now, you're not." He pushed open the door and cool nighttime air hit them. He did a quick examination of the area outside to make sure everything was clear. Just as they stepped onto the sidewalk, a black SUV pulled to a stop and one of his agents stepped out.

Denton led Elle to the backseat, opened the door and gently prodded her inside. He climbed into the front seat and did another scan of the area for danger. Nothing appeared out of place. Without wasting any more time, he pulled away.

Elle leaned between the two front seats. "Who was that who drove the SUV to the door?"

"Sit back and put on your seat belt. And that was one of my men."

Her harness clicked in place. "You had some of your men at the event tonight? I thought my father only hired you?"

"He did. But I always plan for the worst. It's a good thing I did."

The suburbs and strip malls of Virginia Beach blurred past them as Denton escorted Elle away from the Convention Center. He let silence fall while the reality of the situation sank in for Elle.

The person behind these threats was brave. Coming to an event like this and sneaking into Elle's dressing room where they could easily be caught showed a lot of brazenness. The suspect was clearly bent on making Elle shake in her boots.

But despite the threats, Denton would make sure that all this ended well. He'd see to it that nothing happened to Elle.

"Where are we going?" Elle's voice sounded quieter than usual as it drifted from the backseat.

"To your parents' house."

"But they took pictures of me there. Is it safe to go back?"

"Those pictures were taken with a telephoto lens. Most likely, the photographer wasn't even on your father's property—not directly, at least—when those pictures were snapped. My men are going to canvas the perimeter tonight. We're stepping up security."

Silence stretched for a moment, until Elle finally whispered, "Denton, I'm scared."

He softened his voice. "I know, Elle. Let me do the worrying, okay? That's my job."

In the rearview mirror, Denton saw her nod, but her eyes didn't look convinced. She hunkered down in the backseat, just as he ordered. He glanced in his rearview mirror again, this time at the road behind them. Though it was dark outside and an array of headlights glared behind them, his gut told him they were being followed.

He watched the vehicle behind them, noting that it was keeping pace with them at a close clip. He needed to figure out if they were being tailed. He switched lanes and noticed the vehicle behind them did, also.

"Your seat belt is on, right?"

"Of course. Why?"

"Because this ride is going to get a little crazy." He pushed on the accelerator and shot into the right lane of the interstate, swerving onto an exit ramp.

"What are you doing?"

"I'm making sure we're not being followed. Stay down."

Elle's eyes widened just before she disappeared behind the

seat. His gaze went to the rearview mirror again. The head-lights were still there.

He zipped down the right lane of the highway. The vehicle behind them was so close now that Denton couldn't even see the headlights except for the rays that illuminated up from his bumper.

A red light waited ahead. He couldn't stop. Not now.

As the intersection approached, he didn't slow. He re-mained in the right lane, prepared to turn. When he reached the cross road, he jerked the steering wheel to the left, nar-rowly missing the oncoming traffic. Horns blared. Tires skid-ded. People yelled.

But everyone was safe. For the moment, at least.

Elle's high-pitched voice rose in the backseat. "What are you doing? Are you trying to get us killed?"

Denton watched as the SUV behind him threw on the brakes then skidded to the right.

Denton breathed easier. He'd lost them. For now. It would only be a matter of time before those men found Elle again.

Would they be this lucky next time?

FOUR

Reality embedded itself deeper and deeper as Elle gripped the edge of her seat so hard that her knuckles began to ache.

Agony awaits.

What did they mean by agony? What had these men planned for her?

The thought of death alone was scary enough. But to think about dying slowly, painfully, was enough to make panic begin to quake inside her.

She'd heard stories about people who'd been tortured. She'd always felt immune from the reaches of people who inflicted pain like that. But was anyone immune? Not really. It was simply that no one wanted to face the reality that something like that could happen to them.

Would even Denton be able to protect her? She believed the man to be capable, but no one was superman. All it would take was one wrong move.

She was right with God. She wasn't afraid of being dead. It was the dying part that got to her.

Finally, the vehicle seemed to slow and merge in with the flow of traffic. Her heartbeat eased some. The reality of the situation wouldn't leave her, though.

"Where'd you learn to drive like that?" Her voice had lost

any sense of perkiness it may have once had. Even with some effort, her pitch still sounded dull.

"I've had some training."

"What did you do before you worked for...what did you call it? Eyes?"

"That's right. Iron, Inc. is our real name, but everyone who knows about us calls us Eyes. I was a Navy SEAL for a while before the CIA recruited me."

"You were a spook?"

He smiled. "I'd tell you what I did for them, but then—"

"Let me guess, you'd have to kill me?"

"Smart lady."

She pushed herself back into the seat, her head beginning to pound as her limbs throbbed. That's what happened when adrenaline pulsed through her uncontrollably only to wither over and over again, she supposed. "Tell me about Eyes."

"A friend of mine, Jack Sergeant, started it several years ago. We do contract work, a lot of it for the Department of Defense, but we also work for local law enforcement agencies, as well as for citizens."

"I see. It sounds dangerous."

"Depends on the job."

"And what's your job there? Bodyguard?"

He chuckled. "No, I'm actually the assistant director."

"This must be serious if my dad hired the assistant director."

Denton's nonanswer seemed to be answer enough. Elle chewed on her thumbnail as they rolled down the road. Everything still seemed so surreal. Was this really happening? Maybe it was a nightmare and she'd wake up any time now.

She knew she wouldn't, though.

"Why don't they just ask for money?"

Her question seemed to surprise Denton. "What was that?"

"If they know I'm a senator's daughter now, why don't

they simply demand money? Isn't that what they're ultimately after? Why go through all this trouble to threaten me?"

"That's the question we're trying to answer, Elle."

They pulled onto the lane that led to her family's home. Tonight, the drive seemed eerily quiet. It was just because everyone else was at the reception, she told herself. It's where she should be.

Denton pulled up at the gate. Elle unbuckled her seat belt and leaned forward, feeling like safety was finally in sight. "Just pull forward and I'll wave to Jimmy. He'll open the gates for us."

Denton crept closer, but the gates didn't move.

Denton gripped the steering wheel. "You think he stepped away for a minute?"

"I doubt it. He's very dedicated to his job."

Nausea churned in Elle's gut. Something was wrong. She knew it. She could tell that Denton knew it, too.

He put the car into Park and pulled the gun from its holster beneath his jacket. He glanced in the backseat at her. "If anything happens to me, Elle, I want you to get into the driver's seat and get out of here as fast as you can."

Reality hit her like cold water in the face, causing her hands to tremble. "Denton, why are you talking like that?"

"Just do what I say, okay? Lock the doors when I get out."

"You're scaring me. Can't you just stay in the car? Call the police?"

He locked gazes with her. "Everything's going to be okay. I just need to check things out."

She nodded, even though all her instincts told her to do just the opposite.

"Did you hear me, Elle?"

She started to nod again, but instead cleared her throat. "Yes, I hear you."

Denton climbed from the vehicle and Elle hit the lock button almost before he was even out. Her heart raced as she watched him approach the guard station. Where was Jimmy? Why wasn't he at the gate like he always was?

Lord, I don't even have the words for the situation. My heart is just crying out to You. You know my prayers even when I don't.

With the skill of someone who had done this a million times before, Denton checked his surroundings, moving swiftly but purposefully.

Capable. Denton was capable, Elle reminded herself. It would be different if it were her out there looking for Jimmy while trying to keep one eye out for the bad guys.

As he disappeared inside the guard house, she held her breath. Minutes ticked by. Or perhaps it was actually seconds that felt like minutes.

Was Denton okay? Was Jimmy inside? And was Jimmy okay? Questions raced through her head so fast she could hardly keep up.

She didn't release her breath until she saw Denton emerge. He strode over to the SUV and tapped on the window until she unlocked the door. He slid inside.

"Well?" She tried to read his gaze but couldn't.

"Jimmy's been shot. I called the police. They're on their way."

"Shot? Will he be all right?"

"He's dead, Elle."

Elle's parents' lawn became a jungle of emergency response vehicles, trolling firefighters and police officers and dizzying flashing lights. The police had already questioned both Denton and Elle, and now the crime scene unit was collecting evidence. Elle's father and his entourage had arrived and now milled around, only adding to the confusion.

Elle looked pale as she stood on the massive porch, her

arms wrapped over her chest and a dazed look in her eyes. Denton wrapped up a conversation with her father and hurried across the darkened lawn toward her. She was a sight to see, that was certain. Even in the middle of the terrible circumstances he'd already seen her experience, she maintained a certain dignity and strength that Denton had to admire.

She didn't turn his way as he strode up the stairs and to her side. Her eyes had that faraway look still. Denton put a hand at her elbow, trying not to jar her. "Elle, I need your help." He needed to distract her from her thoughts, also.

Some of the focus returned to her gaze as she angled toward him. The tight hold of her arms over her chest loosened slightly, but her eyes still looked strained. "Of course. What do you need?"

"To start with, I need a list of your father's staff, his interns, his campaign volunteers—everyone."

"Do you plan on checking out all those people? Because we have hundreds of volunteers right now. The election is only three weeks away."

"We'll vet them all if we have to."

She stared at him a moment before nodding, shades of blue and red from the police cruiser in the distance lighting her face. "I'll get a list for you if you think it will help."

He nodded toward the front door. "I'll also need a tour of the house and a list of anyone staying there."

She blinked. "A tour?"

"It's going to be your temporary home and mine until we know you're safe. I'm bringing in another agent to guard the perimeter at night and someone else to shadow your father. We can't take any chances."

She swallowed, still appearing stiff. The shock of finding Jimmy hadn't worn off yet. The death of a loved one sometimes never wore off. Denton knew all about that.

Elle stepped toward the door, her lithe figure somehow

looking weighed down with a million stones at the moment. "Why don't I give you that tour now? It beats standing out here and staring at the chaos and destruction around me."

Exactly. "Sounds like a plan."

They walked into the massive house—seven thousand square feet, from what Denton had been told. Two wings and no expense spared. Apparently, the senator had won several big lawsuits as a trial lawyer that afforded him any luxury he might want.

They paused in the two-story marble entryway, and Elle pointed to the left. "In the south wing, we have the kitchen, living room, my father's office, two other rooms we use as offices when working here and a library."

"Do you work here a lot?"

She shrugged. "We have campaign offices throughout the state, including one in Norfolk. But working here is convenient and the space is ample."

"Your best option right now is to work here until these men are caught."

Her expression remained neutral. "That's what I concluded, also. That's no problem. I can do my job from here with relative ease." She sucked in a deep breath and slowly released it, as if regaining her composure. "Oh, and speaking of work, Bentley stays in a bedroom upstairs, also."

"Bentley stays here?"

"Not all of the time, but if he's in town with my father, he's around enough that he's practically family." She stepped in the opposite direction. "In the north wing we have the family's bedrooms, some guest suites, a racquetball room and an exercise room."

"I'll need to stay somewhere close to your bedroom."

"The bedroom beside mine should be comfortable for you."

They moved through the house, and Denton found out her schedule for the week—which included a huge fund-raising gala in two days. The mere thought of it caused Denton's muscles to tighten. Big crowds, a difficult-to-control environment and at least two men who wanted Elle dead—not a good combination.

Elle paused by the kitchen, her luminous eyes glancing up at him. He saw intelligence in their depths…and fear. "I don't have to go to the gala."

"No, you should go. It will take some planning on my part, but we can make it work."

She sagged against the wall a moment. "None of this seems real, you know."

"We're going to get through this, Elle."

She seemed to hesitate a moment before nodding. "Yes, we will. Now, if you don't need me for anything else, I'll show you to your room and then get some sleep myself. I have a busy week, as you're going to soon find out."

"Remember—your safety is more important than your father being reelected."

"I know." She looked off in the distance. Denton wanted to do something—anything—to help wipe away her worries. But there was nothing he could do except offer his protection…and pray.

He'd be doing a lot of praying until these guys were behind bars.

Even in the midst of cardboard alphabet letters, multiplication tables and twenty-five giggling second-graders, Denton stayed glued to Elle's side. No, an elementary school wasn't the most likely place for someone to come after Elle. But Denton couldn't be too careful.

Senator Philips sat at the front of the classroom, reading a book to the eager students seated in a semicircle around him. Elle stood at the back of the room with the rest of her father's handlers. Her gaze fluttered between her BlackBerry and her father.

Denton had encouraged her to stay home and to lay low, but Elle wanted nothing to do with that. The police had found no clues, come up with no answers. Nothing was known except that an innocent man's life had been taken.

Jimmy had been shot by a Glock, right through the skull. The rest of the perimeter was clear. But someone had obviously been trying to send a message—a deadly message. They'd gotten to Jimmy. Denton would make sure they didn't get to Elle.

"'The end.'" Senator Philips closed the book and grinned at the children around him. A newspaper photographer snapped a picture, capturing the moment. Great publicity shot, which Denton was sure was exactly what Elle hoped for.

Elle tucked her phone back into her purse. "I think we're all done here. My dad has some meetings he needs to attend for the rest of the afternoon."

"So what else is on your schedule?" They began walking with the entourage down the hallway. A menagerie of black SUVs waited out front. Denton made sure that one of his best men would be driving the one Elle rode in. He wouldn't take any chances. The stakes were too high, the threats too ominous.

"I've got to answer some emails." She glanced up at him and, just for a moment, Denton thought he saw a glimpse of vulnerability. As quickly as it appeared, it vanished. "Other than that, I'm not sure. I just need to keep myself occupied."

"Why is that?"

"Because if I don't, my anxiety might get the best of me."

She wasn't too proud to admit her fears or weakness. That was a good sign. That vulnerability reminded him a bit of Wendi, though she hadn't let very many people see that side of herself. It had been a privilege reserved for those closest to her and seeing it had always had a way of making Denton feel special.

His heart panged as he remembered her bright smile, a smile that had been dimmed by too much chemo and radiation and pain. He missed that grin. No, there would never be anyone else like Wendi. That's probably why he'd contented himself simply to casually date women who he saw no future with. It seemed safer that way.

He stopped by the front doors and waited for Senator Philips to finish shaking hands with the principal. His slick-soled shoes clacked against the floor as he headed toward them.

"Elle, don't forget. You need to listen to Denton."

Elle's lip pulled down in a frown. "He's my bodyguard, not my babysitter, Dad."

"I know. But I know how stubborn you are. This is no time to try and prove yourself. Lay low."

She offered a curt nod. "I will."

Senator Philip's gaze fell on Denton. "Keep an eye on her."

"Yes, sir."

He motioned to the three others with him to follow him outside. Denton saw the red on Elle's cheeks, could tell she didn't like being addressed like a child—probably ever, but definitely not in public. Her father probably had good intentions, just poor delivery. He took her arm. "You ready?"

She nodded, and they stepped into the crisp outdoors. A chilly autumn wind swept against the stoop and ruffled their hair. His gaze surveyed the landscape. Nothing appeared out of the ordinary. Still, he kept a brisk pace as he led Elle to the SUV and secured her inside, then he joined her.

The driver pulled away. "Where to?"

"Back to your parents'?" Denton asked.

Elle clicked her seat belt in place. "I really need to swing by my place and pick up a few things. Especially since everyone insists that I can't stay there right now."

"Your parents' house is safer," Denton stated.

Lines tightened at her eyes. "Of course."

"Just give me your address and we'll go there."

She identified the street before looking out the window, a certain melancholy seeming to fall over her.

"Elle?"

She glanced at Denton, the sparkle gone from her gaze. "Yes?"

"I'm not going to tell you what to do."

Her eyelids fluttered down a moment, some of the hard shell she tried to put on disappearing when she looked back up. "What do you mean?"

"I mean, my job is to protect you. But you're a grown woman. I'll respect your decisions—unless I see a bullet flying through the air."

She stared at him a moment before answering. "Thank you. I appreciate that."

Fifteen minutes later they pulled up to a modest condo located on a golf course in Virginia Beach.

"Stay in the car while I check things out. Please."

Elle nodded, and he slipped out. He used Elle's key to unlock the door and slip inside. He was surprised at her soft and feminine decorations. She always came across as so professional, but her home showed a different side of her. He'd pay attention to that later, though. Right now, he needed to check everything out and make sure it was safe.

Once he'd swept the area, he went back to the car for Elle. She stepped inside and deposited her purse on the honey-colored dinette. Her eyes scanned the place with obvious unease.

"What's wrong?"

"Something feels different." She stepped toward her living room, her brows furrowed.

"What?"

"I don't know. It's just a feeling. You know, that instinct that something has been moved." She whirled around to him. "Did you move anything?"

He shook his head. "Not a thing."

"I'll put my finger on it eventually."

"Let's get your things and get out of here." He nodded toward the door, not liking the implications of what Elle said. What if someone had been in her condo, not to harm her but to take something—or plant something? Why would someone do that?

"I'm not going to argue with you there." She disappeared into her bedroom.

Denton lingered in the doorway, close enough to keep an eye on her, but distant enough for privacy. His gaze wandered the wall of pictures beside him. Elle with her parents. Elle with some girlfriends. An older picture of Elle with another girl when they were probably fourteen or fifteen years old. No pictures of Elle with any men, which seemed to confirm his initial impression that she was single. Not that it mattered to him. He wasn't looking for a serious relationship—any relationship, for that matter. Despite that, his heart still lifted slightly at the realization.

Elle charged from her room, walking toward the living room like a woman on a mission. "I think I know what's different."

Denton followed at a close clip behind her. She stopped at an end table and picked up a picture frame holding a snapshot of her and the senator. With a shaky finger, she pointed at it. "This is my frame but that's not my picture." She scrambled to remove the backing.

Denton put his hand over hers. "Let me." He didn't know what might wait beneath that picture. It could be an airborne disease, for all he knew. Or it could be nothing.

Carefully, he slipped off the back of the frame. His heart

raced as he waited to see what waited underneath. He blinked. Nothing. Except a picture of Elle hugging her father.

"Where'd my picture go? Why would someone take it?"

"What was the picture of?"

"My sister."

"Your sister?"

Elle wiped the corner of her eye, obviously trying to conceal the fact that she was crying. "She's been dead for six years."

"I'm sorry, Elle."

"It was my favorite picture."

"Do you parents have another copy?"

She wiped her eyes again before wrapping her arms over her chest. "Probably. I'll ask them."

"Where did someone get this snapshot?"

She shrugged. "Anywhere. It's on my dad's official campaign website."

"Of course," he muttered. "You have a paper bag?"

"Under the microwave."

He walked into the kitchen and pulled out a lunch-sized bag to slip the frame into. "I'm going to have this tested for fingerprints. I'm pretty sure they didn't leave any, but I want to make sure."

She pulled in a deep breath, her face pale and her voice on the edge of fragile. "This feels like... I don't understand why someone would do this."

He resisted the urge to touch her, to try and comfort her. It wasn't his place. But he hated to see her struggling as she was. He stuffed his free hand into his pocket instead. "You witnessed a horrific crime. Sometimes people are just sick. They want someone to pay for what happened. They're playing a game, basically."

She swallowed and nodded. "Let me finish getting my stuff and let's get out of here."

He slid the frame inside the bag. His instincts were ramped. Someone had stepped up the game. Whatever it was they wanted, Denton had a feeling they were sick and twisted enough to not let anything stand in their way.

FIVE

Elle's thoughts were getting the best of her as she stared out the car window. What a whirlwind. More like a nightmare. How had her life gone from orderly to chaotic?

Joshua 1:3-9 ran through her mind.

"I promise you what I promised Moses: Wherever you set foot, you will be on land I have given you.... No one will be able to stand against you as long as you live. For I will be with you as I was with Moses. I will not fail you or abandon you."

The verse had been her grandmother's favorite, one that she quoted to Elle over and over. *I will not fail you or abandon you.* Certainly God wouldn't let her down now, even if it sometimes felt like that when she relied on her feeble, human understanding of circumstances.

"How about we go grab a bite to eat?"

Denton's voice cut into her thoughts, and she sat up straighter. "I'd love to."

"One caveat. I get to pick the place."

"It's a deal."

She looked a moment at the passing landscape. Though they lived in Virginia Beach, they were far from the hustle and bustle of the area's more urban sections. Out here, there were acres and acres of fence-lined lawns, complete with horses and plenty of trees. It was a great place to live…most of the time.

"I know that picture meant a lot to you, Elle. What happened to your sister?"

She cleared her throat. "She was kidnapped. The kidnappers demanded a ransom. We were advised not to pay it. A week later, the police found my sister's body."

"I'm sorry, Elle. Did they ever catch who did it?"

She nodded. "A few weeks later they caught a break. One of the hairs found on her matched someone they had in the system. He claimed his innocence, but the evidence said otherwise."

"At least he's behind bars now."

"My dad used to be a judge. You probably know that, though. Anyway, he made quite a few people mad. He always seems to be a target. Even before he was a judge, he was a lawyer and he defended some pretty shady characters at times. I guess we should be used to this life."

"No one wants to get used to being a target. No one should have to, especially you. You didn't sign up for a life in politics. You were born into it."

"I choose to work for my father. My sister—Emily—she didn't choose any of this. She was barely a teenager. She'd just finished dance class when a man pulled up outside and told her our dad had sent him to pick her up. People told us that she tried to step back, to get away, but the man grabbed her and pulled her into his car."

"It must have been awful for your family."

"Beyond awful. My mom still goes to counseling for it. And my dad…he just works. All the time."

"And you?"

She swung her head up. "Me? I guess I'm like my dad. I stay busy. I worry about Mom." She touched the necklace at her throat. The emblem there seemed to burn into her skin.

A few minutes later, they pulled into the gravel parking lot beside an old building with a hand-painted sign that read Fred's Seafood. Elle had seen the place before, but never bothered to try it. She stared for a moment at the peeling paint on the building's exterior and the flashing sign in the window letting everyone who passed know they were open.

Denton seemed to sense her hesitation. "It's great. I promise. Don't let the outside fool you."

The driver pulled to a stop by the front door, and Denton helped her out of the SUV. Staying close—close enough that she could smell his citrusy aftershave—he ushered her inside the dimly lit establishment. A few people called out hellos as they stepped onto the stained linoleum floor.

One of those places where everyone knew your name, Elle thought. The notion seemed foreign, yet welcome. Denton pointed to a booth in the corner and an older gentleman only visible through the service window into the kitchen nodded approval. Denton slid across the ripped upholstery, sitting where he could face the door.

Elle sat down across from him, resisting the urge to wipe her finger over the table to make sure it was clean. It wasn't that she was a snob. She just liked the familiar places where she knew what to expect, perhaps more than she should. Still, trying new things was good for the soul. She needed to get out of her comfort zone more often.

She glanced around the place and released the breath she held. The building and furniture may be old, but the place itself had more of a homey feel to it than she'd originally expected. The other patrons seemed to mind their own business, and a mix of murmured conversations and clattering silverware filled the air. Elle looked back at Denton, who appeared to be watching her as the edge of his lip tugged upward. She ignored his amusement. "You come here a lot?"

He rested an arm on the table and grabbed a menu to hand her. "Every week if I can."

She grasped the laminated piece of paper and paused. "Really?"

He grinned, way too handsome for Elle to feel comfortable. "Our headquarters isn't too far from here so it's a favorite with all the guys at work. I know it looks like a dive, but they catch the seafood fresh every day and the menu is never the same because of it." He leaned closer. "Not your kind of place, I take it?"

Her gaze scanned today's selections before locking on Denton. "I'm really not as much of a snob as you might think, Mr. Denton."

He tilted his head. "Mr. Denton? You're making me feel old. And for the record, I don't think you're a snob at all. You seem like a five-star-restaurant kind of girl, though."

"The truth is that I love a good cheeseburger every once in a while. Not the expensive kind, either. The kind you get at a drive-through. You'll have to excuse me if I seem antsy. I'm just on edge."

His grin slipped. "Understandable."

"Isn't your driver coming in?"

"He's a bit of a health-food nut, so he always brings his own lunch. I think he's catching up on emails while we eat in here."

Denton's eyes roamed the room. Even though he looked relaxed, he was obviously still on guard. Good. Elle appreciated being with someone competent who took his job seriously, especially when her life was on the line.

A twenty-something waitress came and smiled widely at Denton, fluttering her eyelashes. "Hey, Mark. Good to see you in here again. It's been a few days. I was getting worried that you'd forgotten about us."

"Nah, just been busy. You know you guys are the best-kept secret in this area. How could I forget about that?"

She giggled. "We've got a seafood platter today that I think you're going to love."

"I'll take it."

The waitress turned to Elle and her smile slipped some. "How about for you?"

"Catch of the day. Broiled. Salad on the side with no croutons."

As soon as the waitress stepped away, Elle raised an eyebrow at Denton. "Now I know why you really come here."

He chuckled and shook his head. "It's not like that."

Elle wasn't so sure about that. He was good-looking, charismatic and had a smile that could win over anyone. He probably left a long line of broken hearts wherever he went.

It was a good thing Mark Denton wasn't her type.

Okay, he was totally her type, but what she wanted and needed were two different things. They had to be, for the sake of her emotional well-being.

She laced her hands together on the table and locked her gaze with Denton. "So, you know a lot about me now. How about you? How long have you worked for Eyes?"

"Four years." He leaned back, an arm casually draped across the top of the booth. "I met the company's founder when we were both SEALs. I went on to work for the CIA. When Jack decided to open his own paramilitary operation, he asked me to join his efforts. I did, and, as they say, the rest is history."

"Sounds like quite the operation you guys have going."

"Never a dull moment."

"You must like that kind of life. Full of adventures, taking risks, dodging trouble."

He grinned. "I'm not James Bond, if that's what you're implying, nor do I aspire to be." He shrugged. "I think what we do is important. I think I'm good at what I do. So it's a nice marriage of sorts."

Yeah, Elle had seen his type before. Been engaged to his type before, even. Risk-takers weren't her match, that was for sure. She needed the safe type, the type who were happy with what they had and not always looking for the next rush of adrenaline.

The waitress set a seafood platter in front of Denton and some broiled flounder by Elle. She lifted a quick prayer before unrolling her silverware. She looked up and noticed Denton studying her.

"What?"

"I knew there was something different about you."

"Because I pray?"

"Yeah, because you pray. In public. When you don't have to. I like that."

She raised her fork. "My family grew up only going to church on holidays. But when my sister was kidnapped, my world was turned upside down. I knew I had to trust in a higher being or I'd never find any true hope in this world. The more I studied the Bible, the more I realized that I really believed in God with all my heart—not only because I wanted Him to answer my prayers. I wanted to know Him more because of what He did for me on the cross." She wiped her mouth. "How about you?"

"I was kind of wild for a long time. A party boy, some might say. But after I met my wife, she taught me that there was a lot more to life."

Elle blanched. "Your wife?" Elle hadn't seen him as the marrying type, much less as the *married* type. How had she missed that?

"She passed away two years ago." Elle didn't miss the shadow that fell over his gaze. He'd loved her, and Elle knew all his pain hadn't subsided. Did it ever when you lost a loved one? "I'm sorry. I had no idea you were married."

"Why do you sound so surprised?"

She shook her head, flustered for showing her emotions so easily. "I just…I just didn't expect that."

"I don't seem like the marrying type?"

"Honestly? Not exactly."

He shrugged. "I'll take being married any day to being single."

Elle paused from eating, leaning back slightly so she could soak in the answer to her next question. "Really? What was so great about it?"

"Those were the happiest days of my life. Even with our ups and downs—and we had them—marrying Wendi was the best thing I've ever done." His words sounded sincere, honest and down-to-earth.

Elle's heart thudded. She'd lost hope in having her own *happy ever after,* of finding a good man who believed in forever. She cleared her throat. "That's sweet."

"I mean it." Denton's gaze was unwavering and grounded.

Elle's throat burned with some strange emotion she couldn't identify. "I believe you. I just wish I had that much confidence."

Denton put down his fork and straightened, his eyes narrowed. "Funny, because you seem like the marrying type."

In an effort to retain her composure, she took another bite of her food. The fish was cooked to perfection, she had to admit. Too bad they weren't talking about the food anymore. She swallowed and wiped her mouth, noticing that Denton still waited for her response. "I haven't seen that many examples of happy marriages."

"That's a shame."

She had to change the subject and find a way to not talk

about herself. "What happened with your wife, if you don't mind me asking?"

He shrugged. "It's okay. She's in a better place now and isn't suffering anymore." He paused a moment. "She had brain cancer. We tried everything—surgery, chemo, radiation. Nothing helped. They were all just temporary fixes, I suppose. The last couple weeks before she died were the worst."

Elle's throat burned still. "I can't imagine what that would have been like. I'm so sorry."

"Being married makes you grow up fast. But having a spouse with a terminal illness really shows you what you're made of. I'm glad I was able to be there with her. It was another reason why I wanted to work for Eyes. The flexibility of my schedule let me stay home with her when she needed me."

"How long were you married?"

"Five years. Not long enough." He leaned forward. "You ever been married?"

She shook her head, probably a little too hard. "No. I came close, but thankfully I saw the light, so to speak."

"About your fiancé or about marriage in general?"

She shrugged. "Maybe both." Her cell beeped and she picked it up, saw that Bentley was calling. "Saved by the cell." She smiled before answering. Her smile quickly faded as her father's chief-of-staff came on the line.

"Elle, we have a problem. A big problem."

Her back muscles instantly tightened. "What's going on?"

"Someone hacked into our server again. This time they sent out a letter to everyone on our donation list."

"What did it say?"

"Nothing. It was a picture of your father."

"What kind of picture?" She held her breath as she waited for his response.

"A picture of your father with another woman."

Elle closed her eyes. "What do you mean exactly?"

"You're going to want to see it for yourself. The press is going to have a field day with this."

Elle stood, ignoring how she jarred the table and made everything rattle with the action. She grabbed her purse and began scrambling through her wallet for cash. "I've got to get back to the house and start doing some damage control."

Denton appeared at her side, back in bodyguard mode. "What was that phone call about?"

Where was all of her cash? "Someone sent out an email to our campaign subscriber list of my father with another woman."

Denton's hand went over hers. She couldn't deny that jolt that rushed through her at his touch. "I've got the meal covered. Tell me about the email. You think it's the same person who sent you the threatening email yesterday?"

She paused long enough to close her purse and pull it over her shoulder. "Makes sense to me. I thought our IT guys had fixed whatever problem that allowed them to do it in the first place. Apparently not."

Denton threw some bills on the table while still keeping in stride with Elle. She reached the front door and swung it open.

Denton stepped in front of her. "Wait. I know you're upset, but we still need to take precautions."

She looked up, noticing his close proximity, and her heart seemed to stutter out an extra beat. She quickly looked away and stepped back. "Of course."

Denton scanned their surroundings—fairly simple since it was mostly cornfields and patches of trees—and then motioned toward the driver of the SUV. A moment later, the vehicle pulled up to the door and Denton ushered her inside.

As soon as they started down the road, Denton turned toward her. "Tell me about the photos."

Elle pulled up her email on her phone and blanched when the picture popped onto her screen. The image was of her father seated on a park bench next to a pretty blonde woman not much older than Elle. They were both laughing, sitting close enough that people would ask questions, but far enough away that they'd be able to deny anything. Elle handed her phone to Denton.

He studied the picture a moment, his expression unchanging. "Who is she?"

"I have no idea." Elle had never seen the woman before. But her dad had a separate apartment up in Washington, D.C., where he stayed when the senate was in session. She tried to stay as far away from that life as she could.

"Is your dad…?"

Elle swallowed, her throat suddenly achy. "Having an affair? I hope not. Rumors have been circulating for years, though. I guess I always assumed it was better if I didn't know."

He pointed to her phone, compassion warming his eyes. "There could be an explanation for that photo."

She shrugged. "Could be. I won't know until I talk to my dad. I have to say, family issues aside, this is one of the worst things that could happen for his reelection campaign."

"How about for you?"

She grimaced. "Yeah, I'll deal with how it affects me after I process how it affects everything else. I wonder if my mom has seen this yet."

"Will she be devastated?"

Her mom flashed through her mind. "Sadly, probably not. Their marriage has seen better days. Sometimes I think staying together is a political move more than anything else." Elle shook her head. "I'm sorry. I shouldn't have told you all of that. I don't know what got into me. I always try so hard to be careful what I say, to be 'politically correct,' I suppose. Sometimes it feels good just to be honest."

"Whatever you say is safe with me."

Something about his words caused her cheeks to flush. She believed him. And Elle hardly ever believed anyone. Broken promises seemed to be a theme in her life. Yet here she was being protected by a man she hardly knew, and somehow innately she felt certain she could trust him.

It had been a long time since she'd felt that way. The last time she'd let her guard down, she'd ended up devastated. Would it be the same with Denton?

It didn't matter. Denton would be out of her life soon. Once these bank robbers were behind bars, she'd have her freedom back. And with the local police working the case, certainly an arrest would be made before long.

She prayed an arrest would be made before long.

In the meantime, it would be best not to get too close to Denton. His revelation that he'd been married had shocked her enough and showed her a different side of the man. She'd never, ever guessed him to be the family-man type. But maybe that first impression was wrong.

Her phone rang again. Her dad. She sighed before answering. This was one conversation she didn't want to have.

SIX

Denton tried to give Elle some privacy but that wasn't the easiest thing to do in the confined quarters of a moving SUV. He at least had the decency to look out the window as Elle spoke into the phone.

"Dad, this is one of those times I wished I wasn't working for you because I don't want to ask you these hard questions. But I have to. Who is she, Dad?" Elle's voice sounded sharp, tight.

As it should. His own parents had divorced when he was a teenager, and he remembered the agony of watching his family fall apart. No one whatever the age—should have to experience that. It was one of the reasons he'd always vowed to make his marriage his priority.

Denton couldn't hear her father's response. The man did have a reputation for being a womanizer. Denton knew that much from the time he'd briefly been hired by the senator. It was a shame that so many men who had power abused it by treating those around them so poorly. He'd seen it time and time again.

"Why would you let yourself be alone with her, Dad? Even if nothing happened, you know how gossip can start. We're going to have to do some major damage control. As soon as I get home, I'll call all the TV stations—if they haven't already called me on my office line. We'll write up a statement and put you in front of the camera. I need to talk to this Nancy Green, also, before the press gets to her."

Silence lingered as Senator Philips responded.

"I'll talk to you about it back at the house." A moment later, Elle snapped her phone shut and closed her eyes. "This just gets better and better. That woman in the picture? She lives in the apartment beside him up in D.C."

Though Denton would never wish this situation on anyone, at least it provided Elle with a momentary distraction from her other problems. This wasn't exactly the distraction that he'd hoped for, though.

"Who would do this?"

"One of your father's political opponents?"

"They'd deny it if they did." She sighed and looked out the window again.

As they pulled down the lane leading to her home, the driver braked. "Uh, boss, you'll want to see this."

"What is it?" Denton pushed himself between the seats in time to see the commotion at the end of the drive.

"We've got a welcoming committee."

Sure enough, three news vans blocked the entry to Elle's house. Reporters mingled. Camera crews waited to pounce. "Keep going. They'll move out of our way. Elle, stay down."

As they got closer, the news crews spotted them and surrounded the vehicle.

"Is it true that someone's after you?"

"Is your father having an affair?"

"Why would someone want you dead?"

Elle glanced over at Denton. "Great. They already know. That didn't take much time." Her phone rang again. "It's one of the local reporters." She hit the end button. Her phone rang again and again until she turned it off.

Finally, they got through the crowd. The gate inched open and they pulled through, away from the craziness outside it.

"I've never seen it like that before," Elle muttered, climbing back into her seat.

As soon as Elle was safely settled inside, Denton was going to start looking into the background of everyone who worked for Senator Philips. News like this didn't leak on its own. He hated to think that someone close to the family might be behind it all, but he couldn't rest until he knew Elle was safe.

That was the job he'd been hired to execute, and he planned to do just that.

As soon as Denton stepped into the Philips' home, he felt the tension that filled the air. There were no smiles or warm greetings. No, everyone walked around with their back muscles pinched, with serious expressions straining their faces. Their words sounded terse, their glances were brief.

They were in panic mode, realizing that Senator Philips's campaign may have just died a quick death.

Denton hoped that Elle's father was more concerned with the survival of his daughter than he was with the survival of his reelection.

Elle charged forward, breaking through the crowd of advisors, assistants and interns. She seemed to have an internal radar as to where her father was. Denton kept her in sight while assessing the crowd.

Was someone behind these threats in the house right now? Had someone here broken the trust of the family? He'd look into that list Elle had given him of the campaign staff and volunteers. He'd even check into Elle's ex-boyfriends if that would help. He didn't want any stone to be left unturned.

He caught up with Elle just in time to hear her father say, "Bentley's going up to talk to Nancy now."

Elle's hand went to her hip. "Bentley? You sent Bentley?"

Senator Philips shrugged. "I couldn't send you, not with everything going on."

"Dad, Bentley is a great strategist but he's a terrible people person. That was a bad idea."

"I couldn't very well go up there to talk to her myself! The moment I did, a reporter would jump out and snap another picture. Besides, he has a degree in law. He should know how to get the job done."

Elle shook her head, her jaw locking in place. "Where's Mom? I need to check on her."

"She's in her room. She doesn't want to talk to anyone right now." There didn't seem to be any sympathy in his voice. It remained crisp and tight. Was that the true mark of a politician? The ability to always appear plastic and unemotional?

Elle started toward the stairway. "She'll talk to me."

As soon as Elle stepped out of earshot, Senator Philips turned to Denton. He motioned for everyone else to leave the room and shut the doors. Then he pulled down the cuffs of his crisp white shirt. Worry showed in the crinkles at the corners of his eyes. "I'm not convinced that all of this isn't connected."

"If you don't mind me asking, sir, when was that picture taken?"

"Last week."

"Then it can't be the same people. This has to be someone else who's targeting your campaign."

His shoulders sagged slightly, and he paced back toward his desk. "Well, that's a relief, I suppose, at least in one sense. I just want to make sure my little girl is safe. That's my biggest concern right now." Denton was glad to hear it.

"Did you check in with the detectives on the case today? Are there any updates I should know about?"

"They're tracking down a couple leads. They don't know anything definitive yet."

The senator paused, a hand going to his hip. "I heard about someone taking the picture of Emily from Elle's place. What does that mean exactly?"

"I wish I knew. I think these guys are more calculating than we're giving them credit for. They're planning something, and I don't like it."

"I don't understand why they're coming after Elle. They did the crime. They should be running from the police right now, not trying to chase down my daughter."

"Until we understand their motivation, we won't know why they're doing this. Is it just revenge? It could be. But you're right, Elle isn't the one to blame for what they did. The only thing she did was call 9–1–1."

"But then that article ran and they figured out she was a politician's daughter. People have tried to manipulate me by manipulating my family for years. Why they decided to target Jimmy in the middle of all of this, I don't understand."

"Coincidences are rarely that. There may be more at play here than we realize. I'm going to look into all of your staff and volunteers."

The senator froze, his eyes going ice cold. "You think someone on my staff is behind these incidents?"

"I just want to check every lead."

The senator's gaze locked on his. "I trust you won't let anything happen to Elle."

"I'll give up my life to protect her if I have to."

Elle rapped on the door to her mother's bedroom and heard "Go away" from the other side. She pushed open the door anyway. "It's me."

Her mother said nothing, so Elle stepped inside. She spotted her mother sitting in a chair by the window, staring absently outside. The room was dim and too large to feel comfortable. The only light came from the rays of the early afternoon sun that filtered in through the gauzy window shades. Elle crossed the room and lowered herself into the chair across from her mom.

Her mother's face was absent of tears. Her eyes weren't even red-rimmed. But her absence of emotions said far more than weeping would have.

Elle touched her mother's hand, trying not to flinch when she noticed the coolness of her skin. "How are you?"

She continued looking out the window, not breaking her gaze for even a moment. "Another allegation."

Most people didn't see this side of her mother. She appeared so strong whenever she was in public, putting on the perfect facade for everyone watching. "I'm sorry, Mom."

"Marriage isn't all that it's made out to be, Elle. I gave up years ago. I just hate the embarrassment this brings to the family."

Elle's heart lurched. Certainly marriage could be good, couldn't it? Not all unions ended in heartbreak and brokenness. Sadly, Elle was beginning to believe her mom's words more with each passing moment. Nearly all the marriages she'd seen had dissolved over time. *Dissolved* was probably too nice of a word. Most had ended with a tragic—but figurative—explosion.

"I hate that this hurts you, Mom."

"He claims they're just friends. It doesn't even matter."

What did Elle say? What were the right words, words that would bring healing and not pain? "Is it worth fighting for, Mom?"

Her mom jerked her gaze toward Elle. "Is what worth fighting for?"

"Your marriage."

She stared at Elle a moment before scoffing. "I'm way past that, Elle. I gave up hope about my marriage a long time ago."

Silence stretched between them. So maybe that wasn't the

best thing to say. Elle didn't know what was, though. Everything that came to mind seemed like a platitude, and the last thing she wanted was to cause her mom any more pain. She'd had enough of that in her life already.

"What can I do?" Elle finally whispered.

Her mom shook her head. "Nothing. You should go help your dad with damage control."

"He sent Bentley to do that."

"Then go relax. Or try to, at least. All this stress is going to make your hair turn gray prematurely."

Elle had bigger things to worry about than her hair turning gray. She tried to pull herself together as she dragged herself downstairs. Somehow, she'd always seemed to make herself the mediator, the one who tried to smooth things over. She tried to stuff her feelings down deep in order to address everyone else's. But, at the moment, they all threatened to spill out. Maybe it was the allegation against her father or Jimmy's murder or the bank robbery. Maybe a mix of all those things. For some reason, she just felt ready to break.

She sucked in a deep breath and forced a smile as she stepped into her father's office. She felt everyone's gaze on her, but the only person she dared to look at was Denton. His warm brown eyes studied her as they often did.

Was Mark Denton trying to figure her out? Good luck with that.

She cast aside her emotions, her questions, her fear and pulled herself up to full height. "We need to formulate what you're going to say in your statement to the press, Dad." She glanced at her father. "Has anyone heard from Bentley yet?"

Brianna stepped forward, clipboard in hand. "He just left to go up to Northern Virginia a couple hours ago. He should be there in another hour. We're waiting to hear back from him before we proceed."

"Smart thinking. Let's go ahead and draft a statement that we can revise later."

Damage control. Between her rocky family life and her sister's murder, it was almost like she'd been training her entire life to do this job. Sad, but true.

"Brianna, how about if you and I go into my office to work on that. We'll let the rest of the staff worry about how this happened. We'll figure out how to handle it."

They headed down the hall and began working on drafting a press release for the next two hours. Elle tried not to let her mind slip to the issues and worries that kept begging for her attention. She tried not to think about Jimmy and the threat on her life. She attempted to not think about the allegations against her father. But in between writing an official statement, her mind wandered there.

Denton made himself comfortable in a chair by the door, a laptop in front of him. He tapped away, doing something unknown to Elle. Every once in a while he'd scan the room. His gaze would focus outside the window. Still on the lookout for anyone planning an attack.

At quarter past six, her father stepped into the room. Good. Maybe he'd heard from Bentley. She stood from her seat at the paper-covered table, smoothing her outfit as she did so, and stepped toward him. "Do you have an update?"

Her father's grim gaze made her tense. He stood rigid and his breaths seemed to come faster than normal. The news wasn't good, Elle realized. Had the woman in the photo threatened to go to the media? Refused to sign a confidentiality agreement? Implied there had been more to their relationship?

Her dad rubbed his hands together and lowered his head. "Bentley went to Nancy's apartment."

"Okay…"

He swallowed, his Adam's apple bobbing up and down.

"The door was open, but no one answered. When Bentley stepped inside, he saw Nancy on the kitchen floor. Dead. Murdered."

SEVEN

Murdered? That puzzle piece didn't fit with the rest. Denton stood, a sense of foreboding haunting him. "Manner of death?"

The senator's gaze, suddenly weary, locked with Denton's. "Bentley said there was blood. A lot of blood. And a knife on the floor. The police are there now, gathering evidence. Bentley has to stay until they finish questioning him."

"Did he give you any other details?" Denton's mind raced through the possibilities, the connections, the links.

"Bentley guessed, based on the way he found Nancy, that she's been dead…for a couple days. That's based purely on the way he found her, the state of her body. He's not an expert, mind you."

"When was the last time you were up in D.C., sir?" He didn't want to ask the question, but he had to cover every angle.

The senator's gaze snapped toward to Denton. "You're not implying that I'm behind her death, are you?"

"No, sir. But the media might. I just want to know what we'll be up against."

Elle stepped forward, lines evident at the corner of her eyes. "You haven't been up to D.C. in a week, right?"

Her father's gaze shifted ever so slightly. Most people

would have missed it, but Denton didn't. "When did I have time to go up there? Life has been in overdrive lately with the campaign."

The senator had been there. The questions were when and why? Denton would save them for later, when Elle wasn't around. She'd already been through enough. Denton didn't want to burden her further.

Denton grasped Elle's elbow. "It's even more urgent now that we keep you guarded. Three people have died."

Her face lost all of its color. "They're not connected."

"We don't know that."

Her fingers went to her temples again and this time she rubbed her skin there. "That's crazy. Why would a bank robber who's angry with me kill someone who was photographed last week with my father? It wouldn't make sense."

"That's what we're trying to figure out."

Elle shook her head. "You're wrong. There's no connection."

"Elle, everything is a possibility right now."

"Dad—" She stopped midthought and shook her head as if coming to terms with her ideas.

He raised his hands. "I know nothing about this. I told you. I haven't spoken with the woman in a week. I certainly know nothing about her death."

"How would someone know about that photo? It was taken before the bank robbery." She sank into a chair. "This is getting creepier and more confusing by the moment. I don't like it."

Denton sat beside her. "No one does. But we're checking out every angle. The FBI will probably be called in, and they'll put all their resources into figuring this out."

Elle said nothing, but he could tell she was still turning her thoughts over and over.

She was right about one thing—the pieces weren't fitting

together, especially if that photo was taken last week before the bank robbery.

He didn't believe in coincidences. So just what were these madmen doing?

Elle lay in bed, staring at the ceiling. She had too much on her mind, too many unanswered questions and unresolved fears to sleep.

Finally, she threw off the covers and pulled on a robe over her pajamas. Maybe a midnight snack would give her just enough sustenance to help her drift to sleep. If not, at least she'd break out from the prison of her thoughts for a brief moment.

She opened her door and listened. Nothing. Good. Hopefully she could slip out without being heard.

She tiptoed through the hall and down the stairs. In the kitchen, she poured a tall glass of milk and grabbed two leftover cookies. The massive windows in the kitchen—at one time a favorite aspect of the room—now felt intruding and dangerous. Instead of settling at the breakfast table, she tucked her cookies into a napkin and turned to go to the library.

She gasped at the figure leaning casually in the doorway.

Denton. Wearing jeans, a white shirt and a holster around his shoulders. Elle swallowed, her throat suddenly dry. The man had never looked better.

She quickly came to her senses, remembered that he was off-limits, on more than one level. "You wear that thing to bed?" She pointed to his holster.

He smiled. "Maybe."

She held up her snack and shrugged. "I tried to be quiet."

"I'm trained to be alert."

"I should be thankful, then, because it proves you're adept."

"You needed me to prove it?"

She started past him, catching the scent of his cologne. She didn't realize she even liked the smell until that moment. "I didn't say that, but a little assurance is always nice."

"I see how it is. I'm going to have to prove myself to you." He nodded. "I can respect that."

"Don't mind me. I don't trust easily. It comes with the lifestyle."

He nodded toward her cookies. "Hungry?"

"Since you're up, why don't you grab something?"

"I don't mind if I do."

She paused and waited for him to snatch a couple cookies. He popped one in his mouth as they started back down the hallway. "Good stuff."

"Shirley, our cook, makes the best."

"Shirley Black. Fifty-one. From South Carolina. She's worked for your family for fifteen years. Not married. No kids."

"Impressive."

"I know all about everyone in this household, from your dad's advisors to your cook and even the people from the cleaning company who come three times a week."

"You did your research."

"Did you expect any less?"

"Of course not." She veered off into the library, one of the smaller rooms in the house—and one of the few with no windows. That gave her a moment of security, a temporary measure of peace.

She hadn't been in this room for a while but little had changed. Books lined three of the walls and a massive fireplace adorned the fourth. Two couches faced each other in the center of the room, atop an expensive oriental rug.

"I used to love coming in here when I was girl. My sister and I would play library and would take turns as librarian."

Her smile faded as Emily's picture came to mind. What she wouldn't give to have her sister here to reminisce with.

"It was a rough day." Denton sat on one couch, and Elle sat across from him. She set her milk on the table between them before pulling her legs underneath her.

"You can say that again."

"You holding up okay?"

She shrugged, breaking off a piece of her cookie. "Define 'holding up.'"

"Keeping your sanity. Holding on to hope that things will get better. Finding peace in the middle of the storm."

She frowned thoughtfully before taking another bite of her cookie. "I don't know. I know that I don't like living like this."

"Come on now. Is it that bad having me around?" He flashed a winsome grin.

"Believe me, it's not your company that bothers me. It's why you're here. Last week my biggest worry was whether or not my father would be reelected. Now I'd just like to survive to make it to the election. I kind of thought I'd had my quota of crazy in life and that I had some kind of pass for the next decade or so. I guess life doesn't work like that, does it?"

"Wouldn't it be nice if it did?"

"Yeah, it would."

Silence stretched for a moment. Denton leaned forward and picked up a photo album from underneath the table. He flipped it open. Pictures from one of her father's fund-raising galas filled the pages.

Elle's heart twisted at the sight of the pictures. "Dad has a big gala every year. There's one tomorrow, now that you mention it." She shook her head. "It feels like it should be a month until then. Time has gotten away from me."

He flipped the pages. "Looks like fun."

She shrugged as memories tugged at her. She didn't want to remember some of the moments that had transpired at those fund-raisers. They were too gut-wrenching. "It's fun if you like rubbing elbows with people who think they're more important than they are. Don't get me wrong—they're powerful and rich and many of them are generous. But it's all about schmoozing and networking and I'll-rub-your-back-if-you-rub-mine."

"Not your scene?" Denton glanced at her, the glow from the fireplace casting shadows across his gaze. Something about the way he looked at the moment made Elle want to reach up and touch the stubble at his cheek. She kept her hands firmly on her milk and cookies instead.

She shook her head, turning her attention back to his questions and away from his dashing good looks. "No, not my scene. Just a necessary evil."

He grinned and turned another page. "Fancy-schmancy events wouldn't be my scene, either."

"I actually prefer being around small groups of good friends. Crowds make me feel suffocated and slightly overwhelmed."

"You're the opposite of your father, then?"

She let out an airy laugh. "Most would say that. I try to put on a good front, though."

"I don't know. I can see some of the same determination in your eyes. Crowds may not be your preference, but you're good at being surrounded by people." He paused on a picture. He pointed to it before casting her a questioning glance.

Elle caught a glance at the snapshot and froze. The very subject she'd hoped to avoid, the subject that still made her gut squeeze. So much for keeping the conversation at a surface level. She cleared her throat. "I thought I'd gotten rid of all of those pictures."

"Boyfriend?"

She glanced away from the picture and at the fireplace for a moment, watching the flames dance and crackle. Its warmth heated her cheeks and should have made her feel cozy and at ease. Instead, her throat felt dry and achy. She licked her lips before looking back at Denton. "Ex-fiancé, not boyfriend."

"You were engaged?"

"Until about eight months ago. Sometimes I think our breakup hurt my father more than it hurt me. He saw Preston as his protégé, I suppose."

He moved the book away and leaned against the couch, draping an arm casually along the back. "What happened?"

She glanced at him, raising an eyebrow. "Long version or short?"

"Not as many details as you'd give your girlfriends but more than you'd give a stranger."

She had to smile at that. At least Denton didn't pull any punches. She respected that. "Preston and I met at one of my father's fund-raisers. He was—is, I should say—a brilliant businessman. He starts companies then sells them, makes a bundle of money, and moves on to start new businesses. He was fun and exciting. He fit right in with my family and we had a whirlwind romance, as they say."

"There's a 'but' coming."

"Yeah, there's a 'but.' The 'but' is that he lived for the next venture. Not only in his career, but in his relationships. He had what some people would call a wandering eye. I tried to justify it at first, say it was just a guy thing. Then he cheated on me."

"Ouch."

Her heart thudded as she remembered those eye-opening moments when she'd realized their relationship was anything but ideal or perfect, when she'd realized it was filled with heartbreak and that she had to make some decisions that would affect the course of her future.

"Yeah, ouch. Preston apologized profusely afterward and promised to never do it again. I decided to give him another chance and that's when I came across some text messages from other women. Who knows how many women he'd been cheating on me with? One day I realized I couldn't live the rest of my life with someone who acted like that. As much as I treasure forgiveness, it wasn't worth losing my self-respect."

She hesitantly pulled up her gaze to meet Denton's. Her heart pounded in her ears as she waited for his response. Would he feel pity? Would he see her as weak? His gaze held steadfastly to hers.

"Good girl."

Good girl? Had he said "good girl"? She almost wanted to giggle with giddiness. No, he didn't feel pity or look down on her. She tilted her head, admiring his features for the twentieth time that day. There was something about Denton that made her want to soak him in for the rest of her life. "How do you do it?"

He leaned forward, elbows on his knees. "Do what?"

"Get me to talk like that? I value privacy, but you probably know more about me now than anyone else my father has hired."

"I'm honored." His voice sounded velvety smooth and sincere—just the way that made Elle swoon.

She stood and waved a finger at him, trying to resist a smile as she paced in front of the fire and shook her head. "You're good."

He raised himself to his feet and stepped toward her. Elle couldn't help but notice how he towered over her five-foot-six-inch frame. "Why do you say it like it's bad?"

"I've seen your type." She shook her head and let out a shaky laugh, hating the way her pulse raced when he stepped closer. Mark Denton was dangerous—to her heart, at least. "I've got to go to bed."

"So is my type good or bad?"

Elle nodded. "Good night, Denton."

A grin stretched across his face. "Good night, Elle."

As Denton watched Elle walk away, his grin slipped. The woman certainly fascinated him. And surprised him. And made him want to learn more about her. All things he needed to squash. He was hired to protect her, not get involved with her. Besides, he wasn't interested in a relationship. What he'd found with Wendi was a once-in-a-lifetime kind of love. No one ever could take her place.

He flipped off the lights and paced into the kitchen. In the darkness, he stood by the window and let his gaze roam the landscape. He couldn't see much in the nighttime, only a few deck chairs and the outline of some trees.

He paused. Something glinted in the distance. What was that? The glare had come from the tree line. Had he been seeing things? He knew he hadn't. He trusted his instincts.

He pulled his cell phone from his pocket and dialed his man outside. He'd left the agent on patrol around the perimeter of the house. Denton felt better having eyes inside and outside the house. Agent Banks answered on the first ring.

"It's Denton. I want you to check something in the woods south of the house. Something glinted out there. I just don't know what it was. Maybe binoculars."

"I'm on it."

"Check in with me. And treat this as if it's the killer out there. We're dealing with some real sickos."

"Got it."

Denton pressed in the security code and slipped out the back door, his gun drawn and his phone on vibrate. He hurried to the perimeter and scaled the fence. Once in the cover of the woods, he skulked behind trees, trying not to be seen. On the opposite side of the property, he spotted Agent Banks mimicking his movements, a few steps ahead of him.

Just a couple more feet and he'd be there. As he got closer to the area where he'd seen something, he slowed, making sure each of his steps was careful, quiet. He paused behind a tree and peered around it. He saw nothing. Was one of the madmen hiding just out of sight? Were they waiting for just the right moment to send a bullet through the air?

Agent Banks waved him over. He lowered his weapon—but only slightly—as he approached. "What's going on?"

"No one's here, but they were. Look at this."

Denton squatted on the ground and saw the area where some underbrush had been stomped. Something white sticking out from under some vines caught his eye. Carefully, he pulled it out.

His jaw locked in place as the paper came into view. It was a picture of Elle with an *X* over her face.

Just what was someone planning?

EIGHT

Elle had spent most of the day fielding calls from the media and volunteers about everything that had happened over the past three days. Tonight was her father's annual fund-raising gala—the highlight event of his campaign, the one that everyone talked about and that all the big donors came out for.

Would that be the same this year? Would the news of the past few days scare anyone away? And the bigger question—*should* those events scare people away? She'd briefly thought about begging her dad to cancel.

Last year's gala would forever be stained in her memory. It was the night that Preston had proposed to her, right there in front of everyone. When she said yes, everyone had cheered and mumbled about what a perfect couple they were. It wasn't even three months later that she'd found out he was cheating on her. A month after confronting him, she'd found text messages confirming that there was more than one woman.

She'd broken things off. Preston had begged her to stay, insisted that he'd do better. She'd held strong, despite her heartbreak. He'd called nearly every day for the next three months, pleading with her to change her mind until he finally realized she wouldn't give in.

Her heart twisted at the memory. She would never, ever

put herself in that situation again. She'd steer clear of heart-breakers, even if it meant never getting married.

At the moment, she stood in the grand entryway of her parents' home, the silky material of her royal-blue gown swishing at her feet. Her hair, normally wavy, had been shaped by the curling iron and her makeup was patted perfectly in place. She was ready for tonight's gala—physically, at least. Emotionally was another story.

Seeing Preston was bad enough, but couple that with the threats being made and the danger surrounding her, and it was enough to put her over the edge.

She rolled back her shoulders and raised her chin, trying to work out the kinks from working in the office all day. She'd made phone calls, done interviews, answered emails and penned a press release. Keep busy, she'd told herself. That had been her only goal. Without staying on task, her mind would wander to places it had no business going.

A million times, she'd thought about canceling on the gala and staying in. But she would trust Denton to do his job and protect her. She would show the men desperate to claim her life that she was stronger than they thought.

Despite her bravado, her purse trembled in her hand.

Her attention turned toward someone coming down the stairway. She sucked in a breath when she saw Denton decked out in a tuxedo. The normal shadow on his face had been replaced with a clean-shaved smoothness. Every hair was in place, and he had a million-dollar smile as the finishing touch.

She found herself speechless for a moment as he stopped in front of her. At once, she got a whiff of citrus and spices, the scent sweet but masculine.

She cleared her throat, willing her voice to sound even and unaffected. "You look quite dapper."

"Dapper?" He raised his eyebrows, his eyes sparkling.

"I can't say I've ever used that word before." She chuckled. "It just seemed appropriate."

"Well, then may I say that you look quite hot. Smoking hot, for that matter." He straightened, giving his jacket a tug. "Respectfully speaking, of course."

She smoothed the folds of her rich blue gown. She had to admit that she felt like a princess the moment she stepped into the dress. "Don't make me blush."

"You say *dapper* and you blush. You're a treasure."

She swatted his arm. "Stop. You're bad."

"But I mean it."

Oh, he was bad. So bad that he was good. Charming, smooth, adventurous and entirely too handsome.

Basically, he was everything she was attracted to in a man, but nothing she wanted.

He stepped closer and touched the necklace at her throat. Having him so close made her oddly aware of her quickened breathing. His fingers seemed hot against her skin as he rubbed the pendant at her neck. "You wear this all the time. Tell me about it."

The 14K chain had a charm—a golden dove. The piece was simple, but to Elle it was the most beautiful necklace ever. "My grandmother gave it to me before she died."

"It must mean a lot to you."

Elle nodded, the day the necklace was gifted to her rushing to her mind with nearly enough force to bring tears to her eyes. "It reminds me of a promise I made to her."

He nodded. "A promise, huh? Sounds intriguing."

"She was a good woman. I still miss her." Elle pictured her grandmother's regal bearing, one that was balanced with a gentle spirit and a wise countenance. People were intimidated by the woman until they got to know her. Then they realized what a gem she was.

His eyes softened. "I'm sorry."

Elle swallowed, a chill breezing through her when Denton's grasp slipped from the necklace. His hands went in his pockets instead. Elle had to turn her thoughts to other subjects. "Are you sure tonight is okay?"

"My men have been at the hotel all day sweeping the place and setting up the proper surveillance. There are eyes all over the place."

"And you?"

He grinned. "My eyes will be on you."

Suddenly, being around cold-blooded killers seemed safer than being alone with Denton. Safer for her heart, at least. Despite her efforts to stop it, a grin tugged at her lips as she nodded toward the door. "Let's go."

Five minutes later, they rolled down the road. Elle's thoughts continued to get pulled back to the events of the past week. Too much death, she realized with a heavy heart. Too much death. Would she be next?

She couldn't think like that. But she couldn't stop herself, either.

Any minute she expected to hear ammunition slam through the window, to feel a bullet pierce her skin. She waited to feel the SUV swerve, to smell gas and smoke.

"Don't think like that."

Elle jerked her head toward Denton. "Like what?"

"I can see it on your face. Keep your thoughts going down that path and you'll have a panic attack."

She raised her chin. "Maybe I wasn't thinking about danger at all, Mark Denton."

"Mark Denton? You used my full name. What could that mean?" He raised his brows in that playfully arrogant manner that Elle was quickly getting used to. "Then what were you thinking about?"

She shrugged as the landscape morphed from trees to suburban neighborhoods and strip malls. "Maybe I was thinking about political campaigns. Or eating a slice of my favorite pizza at that shop down on the boardwalk. Or seeing that new movie that just came out that all the reviewers are raving about."

"Are you?"

Her smile drooped, and she tightened her grip on her purse. "No, I'm not."

"Tell me about your favorite pizza place."

"They've got this Mediterranean pizza made with pesto and topped with fresh mozzarella, basil, artichoke and mushrooms. It's the best pizza in Virginia, hands down. And when the weather's just right you can sit on one of the benches facing the ocean and that salty air hits you as you're eating. And, just for a moment, everything seems perfect. All because of a slice of pizza." She chuckled, knowing her exaggeration sounded like just that. But what she wouldn't give right now to have one of those carefree moments.

"I'll have to try it sometime."

She pictured herself sitting on her favorite bench at the oceanfront with Denton. The thought made her feel way too dizzy. If she thought a relationship with Denton would ever work out, then she was a fool. Still, she found herself saying, "Maybe."

They passed the rest of the ride by talking about their favorite hangouts and foods and movies. Finally, the SUV pulled to a stop in front of the hotel and convention center where the fund-raising gala was being held. The driver stopped at the front doors, and Denton helped her out of the vehicle, even being careful not to mess up her dress.

Once they got past security, they stood at the ballroom's entrance for a moment, doubt claiming Elle. "So what now?"

Denton took her hand and rested it in the crook of his arm. "Now, you're going to be escorted by a handsome—I mean, dapper—gentleman into the gala, where you'll make an appearance and show everyone how fabulously well you're doing."

"Handsome, dapper and humble. What a combination."

He grinned. "Shall we?"

"Let's."

They stepped into the dimly lit ballroom. Elle found herself inadvertently squeezing Denton's arm—his solid, muscular arm. She scolded herself for noticing. But she had to admit that there was something very reassuring about having him at her side. She shouldn't get used to this, though. He'd be out of her life soon enough.

Her gaze roamed the crowd, and she immediately identified a handful of regulars who never missed one of their fundraisers. Across the room, her mom and dad mingled, looking like royalty in their formalwear. Memories from last year flooded back to her. The night had felt so perfect at the time.

Brianna rushed over to them. "You both look like you just stepped off the pages of *Glamour* magazine. Stunning. Both of you."

"I don't know about me, but I agree that Elle looks fantastic."

Elle ignored the flutter beginning in her stomach and focused on her friend. "How's it going?"

"Everything's running as smooth as the fondant icing on that looks-too-fancy-to-eat cake over there." Brianna paused. "Elle, there's something I need to tell you—"

Before she could finish her sentence, someone stepped forward. "Elle. Fancy seeing you here."

Elle knew the voice without even looking up. Preston. She heaved in a breath, bracing herself for whatever the conversation might hold. "Fancy seeing me at my father's fund-raiser? Good to see you, too, Preston." *Temperance, Elle. Temperance.* That's what her grandmother would tell her to remember. Always be classy, but stand your ground.

He hadn't changed in the six months since she'd last seen him. He was still tall, skinny, blond and traditionally good-looking. Not as good-looking as he thought he was, however. It was hard to believe that it was at last year's gala that he'd proposed to her and they'd talked about forever.

Preston's beady, calculating eyes—eyes that Elle used to think were intelligent and perceptive—turned to Denton. "Aren't you going to introduce me?"

Elle looked up at Denton and saw the curiosity etched in his gaze. "This is..." How did she introduce him? Certainly not as her bodyguard. She could only imagine the questions she'd get then. "This is..."

Denton extended his hand, a winning smile plastered across his face. "I'm Mark Denton."

"Preston Owens, an old friend of Elle's."

The two men shook hands before Preston turned to her. "Elle, I was hoping I might speak to you." His gaze flickered to Denton. "Alone."

Elle shook her head, having no desire to have a prolonged conversation with her ex-fiancé. Nor did she feel comfortable leaving Denton's side with the threats that had been made. "Anything you have to say to me, you can say it in front of Denton. Mark, I mean."

Preston flinched but only for a moment. He drew himself up with an overly confident air again. "Okay then. I just wanted you to hear this from me."

"Hear what?"

He glanced behind him toward the restrooms before turning back with wide grin. "I'm engaged, Elle."

Elle's throat went dry as she processed his announcement. "Engaged? Wow. I don't know what to say. Congratulations."

"She's really great, Elle. I think you'll like her."

She shoved down her emotions, the memories of their time together. "Is she here?"

"She slipped away to the powder room, but I'd love for you to meet her."

"Well, she's one…" What did she say? Lucky? No way. "She's one engaged girl. Good for you."

"I'm sorry about…" He waved his finger back and forth between them. "You know."

"Don't be. The past is the past." And better a brief period of unhappiness than an entire lifetime. She couldn't believe that she'd actually thought the two of them could have a future. She'd lost her sensibilities and vowed to never do that again. Which was why she needed to tamp down her attraction to Mark Denton. They were professionals who were forced to work together and nothing more. No repeat mistakes when it came to relationships.

Preston's eyes turned serious, and any hint of a smile disappeared. "I've turned over a new leaf."

"You don't have to explain to me. Really." In fact, please don't. Especially not now.

He stared at her another moment before nodding and shoving his hands into his pockets. "Okay then. I guess I'll see you around?"

Elle forced a smile. "Yeah, maybe."

As soon as he stepped away, Denton leaned toward her, close enough that they could talk without anyone else hearing. "You really dodged a bullet with him."

She blinked in surprise at his unexpected words. "What are you talking about?"

"He defines *smarmy*. Not the marrying type. Not the type I would even trust in business, for that matter."

"You could tell that in the few minutes you heard him talking?"

He stepped back and looked her in the eye. "I think he wanted you to look jealous or heartbroken, Elle. I don't know who I feel sorrier for—him or his fiancée."

Elle grinned. "I like you, Mark Denton. My dad picked a great bodyguard."

Denton extended his arm. "Shall we mingle?"

"If we must."

Denton had spent the past hour perfecting the act of being the debonair escort of a senator's daughter. He'd stayed by Elle's side, ever the faithful bodyguard. As the night wore on, Elle seemed to relax and enjoy herself more.

Funny, Denton felt the opposite. As the evening drew on, his worry grew.

As Elle paused to talk with someone else, he scanned the area around them. He couldn't pinpoint what it was, but something felt off. Was he missing something?

His sweep of the room didn't give him any answers. Everyone appeared normal as they nibbled on their food, sipped from their stemware and put on airs with each other. A string quartet played soothing strands in the corner. The smell of expensive perfumes mingled with the savory scent of meatballs and chicken teriyaki.

He glanced down at Elle as she spoke, her hands flying through the air as she explained a story to the couple whose eyes were riveted on her. In the dim light, there was something about her that seemed softer than usual. She said she wasn't in her element here, but she looked like a natural as she rubbed elbows with some of the state's most elite citizens.

"You never did introduce us." The middle-aged redhead Elle spoke with glanced up at him with a grin. "Who's this handsome gentleman?"

Denton couldn't be certain, but Elle's cheeks may have reddened. Again. He was sure Elle considered blushing a curse, but he found it tantalizing. Her hand fluttered toward him, coming to rest on his forearm. They'd had this conversation several times already this evening, and Elle seemed more comfortable now with the script. "This is Mark Denton."

The woman's eyes lit up, and her head twisted in exaggerated surprise. "It's so good to see you dating again, Elle. I wasn't sure you ever would after Preston."

Elle's smile slipped, and she opened her mouth before quickly shutting it again.

He slipped his arm around her waist. "Sometimes you have to go through a couple bad relationships to make you realize what a good one looks likes." He winked. "Right, Elle?"

Her cheeks definitely reddened this time before she forced a smile. "Right." She cleared her throat. "Den—I mean, Mark, this is Annabelle Wentworth. She and her family are some of my dad's biggest supporters."

"We just love Senator Philips. We think of him as family."

"Doesn't everyone?" Denton decided to test the waters, see how the woman reacted.

Annabelle grimaced. "Well, not quite everyone. There were some people threatening to protest the event tonight. Thank goodness they didn't show up."

"Protest? Why?"

"One of the senator's votes on finances didn't sit well with them. Such is the nature of politics." Annabelle wobbled her head back and forth, making Denton wonder if she'd had too much to drink. "And then there's that Travis Ambler."

"Travis Ambler?" He knew who Ambler was, but he wanted to hear this woman's take on the man.

"We call him the senator's stalker. He seems to both idolize the man, and resent him for some of his votes. He's one strange bird. If all else fails, there's always Bob Allen, the bottom-feeder running against the senator. Is there anyone with more enemies than a politician?" Annabelle laughed—a little too loudly—and then stepped back. "Well, nice to meet you." Her glance fell on Elle. "We hope to see you around. Both of you." She chuckled as she glided away.

Denton didn't remove his arm from Elle's waist. Their closeness would allow them some privacy as they talked. "What are your thoughts on Ambler?"

She didn't hesitate to look up at him, despite their proximity. "He pops up every once in a while. Sometimes he wants an autograph, other times he wants to protest. Something's not quite right with the man."

Denton only let his gaze graze Elle for a moment before looking around the room again for anything suspicious. Servers with trays perched on their shoulders wove through the crowd, two security guards stood at each set of doors to the room, and the who's-who of the area rubbed elbows. He recognized Bentley and Brianna and several other members of Senator Philips's staff. What was it that was bugging him?

"I think I've made enough of an appearance. Are you ready to go?"

He pulled his gaze away from the crowd for a moment and nodded. "Yeah, let's get out of here. I'll radio my guy to pull up the car."

He placed his hand on her back and led her to the doors of the ballroom. Just as they stepped into the hallway, an explosion rocked the entire building.

NINE

Elle heard the explosion, smelled the smoke. Screams filled the air as people scrambled in a frenzy to find safety. At the far end of the room, flames licked the ceiling, the walls.

Dad.

Dad had been over there. Was he okay?

How about her mother? Where was she when the explosion happened?

She craned her neck, searching for them. All she saw was a sea of people running, grabbing, panicking. The overhead lights went dark and only the dim glow of an emergency light flickered above them. Sprinklers showered streams of water throughout the room.

Denton's arm circled her waist. "We've got to get out of here."

"My parents…"

"We've got men over there helping them. We need to get you to safety."

People pushed, shoved, bustled to get past. Arms grabbed at her, jostling her about.

"Help! My wife! She's trapped!"

Elle would know that voice anywhere. "My mom. We've got to help."

"It's not safe."

She squeezed his arm. "Please."

Denton's gaze met hers, and Elle could see the strain in his eyes. His job was to protect her, but someone else—someone Elle loved—was in danger. She couldn't live with herself if something happened to her mom when she could have helped.

Denton grabbed her hand. "Don't leave my side. Understand?"

She nodded. Denton pulled her through the crowd, toward the fire. Elle's gaze scanned the area, looking for any more signs of danger. All she saw was fear.

The smoke thickened, creeping into her lungs. The acrid smell of burning plaster and metal became stronger. Her hair fell from the twist that held it back, causing wisps to cling to her face.

There. Her mom was pinned underneath a beam as flames shot closer. Her eyes were closed, pain etched into the lines of her face. Dad knelt at her side, tears streaming down his cheeks.

"Mom—" Elle started toward her when Denton jerked her back.

"It's not safe. Stay right with Agent Banks while I help. Understand?"

She nodded, though every part of her felt drawn to her mother. Denton's words made sense. Elle didn't have the brawn to help dislodge the beam.

Despite the number of people fleeing, a decent crowd of people and security worked the area, trying to put out the fire, to evacuate the crowd, to help those injured. Elle stood with Agent Banks by the service door leading to the kitchen. She wrapped her arms over her chest and coughed, her eyes burning. Sweat sprinkled her face from the heat of the flames.

Her poor mom. They had to help her before the flames singed her clothes and then consumed her.

Please, Lord, help her. Help everyone.

Across the room, two men helped a man hobble away, blood gushing from his leg. A woman with a gash on her forehead walked toward the exit, her eyes dazed. Tables were knocked over from where people had scrambled toward safety.

Tears popped into her eyes. What was going on? How had this happened?

Security guards grabbed fire extinguishers and tried helplessly to put out the fire. The flames continued to come, to grow.

A group of men used a table to leverage the beam atop her mother. Touching the metal would sear their skin. Denton had long since abandoned his jacket and tie. His white dress shirt was dirty, the sleeves rolled up, the collar unbuttoned.

Come on. Help her. Please.

But the beam was heavy. They needed more people to help. She grasped Agent Banks's arm. "Please. Give them a hand."

"I have instructions—"

"I know, but I'll be fine. I'll stay right here and won't move an inch. I'll tell Denton that I forced you to go. But please, you've got to help my mother."

He stared at her a moment and then glanced at the group of men working to help her mother. Finally, he nodded. "Don't go anywhere."

"I won't." She bit her fingernail, trying to keep her anxiety under control before it consumed her. They would get her mom out. They had to.

Please, Lord. Be with us.

A hand clamped around her arm. She gasped, but no one heard her over the noise of the room. Before she could turn to see what was going on, someone jerked her backward, toward the service door. *No. No!*

She grabbed the door frame, using every ounce of strength to latch on. But the man behind her was stronger, his strength making her feel like a rag doll. She felt herself being pulled backward, the blackness of the room like an abyss.

Denton! Her gaze shot across the room to where he pulled her mom from the rumble.

In the blink of an eye, she would disappear. She had to do something.

Using all of her strength, she rammed her elbow backward. It connected with her captor. His grasp loosened for a moment. She lunged forward, back toward the ballroom.

The man reached for her, but missed. His hand caught her necklace instead. Her throat squeezed until finally the gold chain snapped.

"Help!" she managed to yell.

At once, Denton darted toward her.

"A man. Grabbed me." She pointed behind her.

"Are you okay?"

She nodded, still gasping for breath.

"Someone stay with her!" he yelled before running into the kitchen. "Don't let her out of your sight."

That had been close. Too close.

Denton glimpsed a shadow at the far end of the room. The outline of man, barely visible in the dim light. As soon as he spotted him, the man slipped out a side-door exit.

"Not so fast!" Denton shoved a service cart out of his way as he took off after him. He dodged around tables and kitchen equipment. His dress shoes fought for traction on the slippery floor, sliding around corners.

The man had a head start, maybe too much of a head start. He had to catch this guy before anyone else got hurt.

As Denton reached the door, he drew his gun from its holster. He swung himself around the corner and paused, scanning in the alleyway. No one.

Where had he gone?

Denton ran down the alley toward the parking lot at the end. The other direction was a dead end. As soon as he emerged from the alley, he froze. Crowds of people stood outside, staring at the hotel with smoke-smudged faces. Fire trucks, police cars and ambulances were all parked haphazardly around the building.

But no fleeing figure.

He jogged toward the edge of the crowd. "Did anyone see a man run from the alley?"

Everyone shook their head no. Of course not. They'd all been watching the building.

Denton stepped onto the hood of a nearby car and searched the parking lot. Where had the man gone?

There was no telling. He'd blended in with the crowd. He'd gotten away.

Denton pulled in a deep breath, resisting the urge to ram his fist into something to subdue his frustration. No, he'd keep his cool.

Right now, he needed to check on Elle again. He should have never left her alone. Maybe he should have insisted that she never come here tonight. But his men had swept the place earlier. How had this happened? He'd figure that out later.

He jogged back inside through the service entrance and found Elle being examined by a couple paramedics. Firefighters had doused the flames, but smoke still lingered in the air. EMTs wheeled away Elle's mom on a gurney.

He touched Elle's shoulder. "How are you?"

She shrugged, her fingers rubbing her throat. "He took my necklace."

"You've got to tell me what happened. Every detail."

She shrugged again. Or did she simply heave in a deep breath? Denton couldn't be sure. He took a blanket from the paramedic and draped it around her shoulders. Though it went against all protocol, he pulled her into a hug. Seeing the range of emotions in her eyes—fear, exhaustion, grief—had pulled at his heart.

Her soft hair tickled his chin and, despite the destruction around them, the sweet scent of vanilla filled his senses. He could drink in the scent all day.

"I want to see my mom," she whispered.

He stepped back and rubbed her arms. "I know the police and probably some other agencies are going to want to talk to you. Let me clear it with the proper authorities, and then I'll drive you to the hospital. Okay?"

Elle nodded.

He had to get to the bottom of how this was happening before someone else was hurt.

Before Elle got hurt.

Elle was grateful for Denton's hand on her elbow as she left her mother's hospital room. Suddenly, she felt weak and exhausted—both emotionally and physically.

"Let's get you home," Denton mumbled as they walked past doctors and nurses scattered in the hallway.

Home. Usually such a comforting word. But now Elle didn't feel safe anywhere. Danger seemed to lurk around every corner.

At least her mother would be okay. She had a broken leg, some cuts and bruises and other minor injuries. All things considered, she was doing just fine. The doctor would keep her in the hospital overnight for observation. Another Eyes agent would guard her room, plus Elle's father would stay with her. Right now, her mom was exhausted and needed to get her rest. Elle had reluctantly left her side.

She caught a glimpse of herself in a mirror in the hospital's lobby. She nearly stopped in her tracks. A zombie. That's what she looked like. Soot all over her face, her hair a tangled mess, her once beautiful dress now torn and tattered.

Denton, on the other hand, looked like he'd been through a disaster but still appeared no worse for the wear. With his sleeves rolled up, his shirt partially unbuttoned and hair tousled, he seemed like a makeup artist had arranged his appearance for maximum effectiveness.

"I look like death," she mumbled.

He squeezed her elbow. "You look beautiful. You always look beautiful."

His words sounded so sincere that she blushed. Any other time, she would have tried to brush back her hair, to slip into the bathroom and clean up some. Not now. Right now, she was ready to get home.

Denton led her into the still night. The black of the nighttime sky was clear and pristine. A full moon hung high above them. For a moment, it didn't seem like something out of her nightmares. For a second, she felt peace.

Then reality flooded back to her. The threats. The danger. The pain already inflicted on those around her.

Denton ushered her into his SUV and then climbed in himself. They sat silently for a moment. He made no move to start the car. Instead, he turned to her. "You need to talk?"

She reached for the empty space at her neck. "I guess there's not much to say."

"Your mom is going to be okay, Elle."

She nodded, her throat suddenly achy with emotion. "I know. But who's next? If not me, then who?"

"These guys are showing the authorities that they're good and we're taking that very seriously. The FBI is being brought in. We'll catch them, Elle. We'll catch them."

Warmth spread from her cheeks down to her fingertips at the reassurance in his words. She shook her head and let out an airy chuckle. He did it. Again.

He tilted his head. "What was that for?"

"For some reason, you have a way of saying things that makes me believe you. I don't know how you do it."

He smiled softly. "I'm glad you believe me."

They began their trip back to the house. Elle reviewed the events of tonight, the scenes replaying in her mind like clips from a bad movie. Her thoughts didn't stop until she remembered the hospital room, until she pictured her mom lying in bed with her leg propped up and a cheap gown replacing her designer one. She remembered her dad sitting at her bedside, grasping her mom's hand.

She cleared her throat. "My dad seemed genuinely concerned about my mom tonight."

"Why do you sound surprised?"

She stared out the window. "I can hardly remember the two of them ever acting like they were in love. Their marriage has always seemed more like a business arrangement."

"Always?"

Elle pulled her gaze from the window to her lap. "I guess before Emily was kidnapped, it was better. We did take family vacations sometimes. We'd rent a house on the Chesapeake Bay and just spend time together as a family. To a lot of people, that would have been boring. But for my family, time together was scarce, so I loved it. After Emily died…" She shook her head. "I don't know. Things just fell apart. Sometimes I don't think we've ever really recovered. We just try to ignore the changes her death has brought into our lives."

"That's tough, Elle. I'm sorry."

"That's why I want to start a nonprofit that will help the families who are living through a kidnapping or abduction."

"Tell me more."

"People who've been through something like having a child taken need more than the immediate help they receive. They need years of help and support. I want to offer that. I want to be able to help them with finances and alleviate a lot of their worries, so they just concentrate on finding their child."

"I like that, Elle. Why don't you do it?"

She shrugged. "I might." She touched her bare neck again. "I promised my grandmother I wouldn't let my fears hold me back. I promised her I wouldn't put everyone else's hopes for me above my own desires."

"You have a problem with doing that?"

"I like being a problem solver, a peacemaker." She shrugged. "I like fixing things."

They pulled up to the estate. The guard house was empty, as it always was at this hour. But it just didn't seem right not to have Jimmy there anymore. Elle had spoken with his family just a couple days ago to see how they were doing. Hanging in. What else could they say? She wanted to stop by and visit, but she didn't think it would be wise. Not when trouble seemed to be following her.

Denton parked outside the garage and they walked to a side door. Now that Elle was back home, she'd enjoy a long, hot bath. She'd scrub away the evidence of the devastation of the evening.

And tomorrow, she'd somehow try to pick up the pieces of her life.

TEN

Elle had tossed and turned all night. She couldn't escape the images of the tragedy that had occurred at the gala. She couldn't stop picturing her mom. She couldn't stop considering the possibilities of how much worse things could have turned out. The fear gripping her heart and mind seemed to be squeezing harder and harder with each passing moment.

Finally, just as the sun began to crack the horizon, she'd thrown her legs off the bed and hurried through her morning routine. When she picked out her outfit and added a splash of her favorite perfume, she told herself her choices had nothing to do with Denton. Yet in between the horrid images that haunted her came moments when her heart warmed. Those were the times when she thought about Denton, about his smile, about the security she felt when he was around.

She had to get a grip on her emotions. Denton was not the type of man she could afford to fall for. Her heart could only be broken so many times before the damage became irreparable. Maybe she was already there. Maybe the men in her life had already ruined her chances for ever falling in love. That's what she had to think, at least, if she wanted to keep her sanity.

Arm's length, she reminded herself, staring at her image in the mirror. That's where she needed to keep Denton.

She successfully avoided him downstairs as she grabbed her breakfast and escaped into her office. She tried to look busy—too busy to talk—for most of the morning. And she was busy. Supporters were calling, inquiring about what happened last night. The press was calling. Volunteers were calling, everyone concerned about her mother and the future of her father's campaign.

Elle's mom had come home from the hospital this morning with a broken leg, a bruised rib and several minor lacerations. It could have been much worse. But it was still hard to see her mom in her injured state. She'd requested a day alone to rest and insisted that her assistant could help her with any needs in the meantime. Elle's father had a meeting in D.C. that he said he couldn't get out of, so he'd headed up this morning and Elle tried to do what she did best—make peace.

She lifted a stack of papers from her desk. Where had Brianna put her notes from last week's meeting? Her friend had requested the day off. She had to get a few things settled with Alex, her soon-to-be ex-husband. Elle tried to get Brianna on the phone one more time but got her voice mail instead. It wasn't like her not to answer her phone. Maybe she was in the shower or blow-drying her hair—doing something where she couldn't hear her Android's Latin-inspired ring tone.

She looked up as Denton stepped into her makeshift office. Her breath caught in her throat—again. She had to somehow will her body to stop reacting every time she saw the man.

He paused in the doorway, his hair still glistening as if he'd just gotten out of the shower. "Morning."

Elle returned the phone to its base and leaned back, reminding herself to remain businesslike and casual…and to ignore her growing attraction for her bodyguard. "Morning to you, too, Denton."

"Listen, I need to use some of the databases at Eyes's headquarters, as well as check on some things there. I thought you might want to come. You know, get out of this house for a while."

Get out of the house? Away from the craziness of the always-ringing phone, away from memories of what could have been? Arm's length, she reminded herself. Still, she heard herself say, "I'd love to."

He tossed her something. "I hoped you might say that. Put these on."

Elle held up the baseball cap and aviator sunglasses. "Really?"

"Yeah, really. We don't want to make it too easy for these guys."

Elle pulled her ponytail through the back of the hat and slipped on the glasses.

Denton smiled. "That's a nice look on you." His smile slipped. "I'll meet you at the inside entrance to the garage in five minutes. Is that enough time?"

"Absolutely."

Ten minutes later, they were cruising down the road. Elle leaned back into the seat, trying to push aside any of the fears that threatened to rear up.

"How'd you meet your wife, Denton?"

"I was at one of the military air shows over at NAS Oceana. She was there with some friends. I saw her and thought she was beautiful. She had a laugh that was contagious and was just so full of joy."

"Let me guess. You walked up to her and got her phone number?"

He chuckled and ran his hand over his mouth. "Not quite. I actually spilled my drink on her."

"On purpose?"

He glanced over at her, a smile playing on his lips as he shook his head. "Of course not on purpose. You think that's how I would try to impress a woman I'm attracted to?"

Elle smiled. This story was not showing the smooth Denton she'd pictured. "I guess not."

"Yeah, so I *accidentally* spilled my drink on her, and I felt terrible about it, of course. I offered to buy her a new shirt, one from the air show. We ended up walking around together and talking afterward. And that was it. We were inseparable after that."

"Your eyes light up when you talk about her, you know."

He glanced over. "You would have liked her, Elle. She was a good person. Honest, kind, sweet, fun."

"I can't imagine losing a spouse. I'm sorry." And she couldn't. How heartbreaking would that be, especially at such a young age?

"The first few months after she died, I would see glimpses of her everywhere. Not actual glimpses or hallucinations. But I'd see the ice cream shop where she loved to get a cone of pistachio cream. Or I'd see an advertisement for a movie featuring her favorite actress. I'd pass the park where I proposed to her. My grief felt fresh again."

Elle's throat burned as she imagined what it would be like to be in his shoes. Devastated. "Has it gotten easier?"

He stared into space for a moment before nodding. "It has. I still miss her. I still miss the life that I thought we were going to have together. But I've accepted what happened. I've come to terms with the assurance that she's in a better place. And I know that she'd have wanted me to move on. So that's what I'm trying to do. I'm trying to embrace life."

"Embrace life, huh? I like that."

"She used to always say that unless you're living with purpose, you're not living at all."

"Sounds like she was a smart lady."

"She was." Denton glanced over. "Thanks for listening, Elle."

"Thanks for sharing."

He looked at Elle again before focusing on the road. "Now is it my turn to ask you a few questions?"

After what he'd shared, how could she say no? "Ask away."

"What exactly was the promise you made your grandmother?"

Of course Denton would cut right to the chase. Elle closed her eyes a moment as the memories absorbed her. "I promised her that I wouldn't be afraid of failing, that I wouldn't let my fears hold me back or be paralyzed by my weaknesses."

"What do you mean?"

She looked down at her hands. "If you haven't noticed, I'm a perfectionist. If I can't do things without a flaw, then I don't do them. It was the reason I never tried to play sports. I knew I'd be so worried about making mistakes that I'd be no good. Instead, I focused on what I knew I was good at."

"Sounds wise."

She shrugged. "In a way, yes. But my grandmother didn't want my fears to hold me back from doing something I really desired."

"You competed in a beauty pageant. You couldn't be sure you'd win. And how about Yale? There were no guarantees."

"It's true, but I knew the odds were in my favor. The truth is that I like staying inside my safe little box. I hate messing up. And I really hate it when others know that I've messed up."

"So you promised your grandmother you'd try something you're afraid of. What's that going to be?"

She shrugged again. "I'm not sure. Maybe when this campaign is over, I'll do some work for a nonprofit. Maybe I'll join the softball team for Parks and Recreation or try singing karaoke for the first time in my life. I don't know."

"Failure can build character, you know."

"You don't seem like the type who's ever failed at anything."

"I fail almost every time I go in the kitchen and try to cook something."

Elle's chuckle faded. "Yeah, but how about big things?"

His smile vanished. "I saved entire villages in Afghanistan from being overtaken by the enemy. I've probably saved the lives of hundreds of people. I don't say that to brag—it's simply the truth. But the one person who was most important to me, I couldn't save."

Elle softened her voice. "It's hard to save someone from cancer. All the brains and the brawn in the world don't help. Not really."

"It didn't stop me from feeling like a failure. I felt helpless." He glanced at her, his face softening some. "But God's brought me through that desert."

Some strange emotional reaction started in her gut and worked itself up to her throat. A fluttering or ache or electricity. A combination of all three? She wasn't sure. She only knew that more than anything she wanted to grab Denton's hand, to pull him into her arms and try to soothe his loss. Instead, she said, "You're a lot more honest and vulnerable than I expected. I appreciate and admire that, Denton."

"Not with the guys I work with. They'd never let it go if I told them those things."

"Sounds like a guy thing." Macho. Tough. Strong. Admitting your weaknesses always made a person sound the toughest, though.

"Speaking of which." He pulled to a stop in front of a massive iron gate with a guard station. Two security officers checked the vehicle before they were allowed to pass through.

Elle leaned forward so she could soak in the paramilitary compound around her. "This is where you work?"

"It's my home sweet home away from home. The headquarters of Iron, Inc."

"Impressive." And it was. The grounds were lush and

green. A large lodgelike building stood in the distance. A group of men in uniform ran in even formation to her left and a rippling lake sat to the right.

"You think the grounds are impressive, you should meet the people who work here."

"Well, I've already met you, haven't I?"

"Are you trying to make me blush, Ms. Philips?"

"It would be nice if the tables were turned for once."

He chuckled and pulled into a parking space. "You're safe here. Maybe you can finally relax—really relax—for a couple hours, at least."

"I'll take whatever I can get."

He nodded toward the front door. "Come on inside, then."

Elle stepped through the front doors and marveled at the design of the building. A two-story foyer with fireplaces on each side, lush leather couches and warm rugs.

"No wonder you like it here. It looks like a five-star resort."

"We try to make it as comfortable as possible." A new voice cut through the air.

Elle turned toward the sound. A tall man with a square face and imposing demeanor walked down the steps. He extended his hand, a welcoming smile on his face. "Jack Sergeant."

"Elle Philips."

"Jack!" Denton and Jack exchanged a hearty handshake. "I didn't think you were back yet."

Jack grinned, his hands going to his hips like an army general surveying his troops. "Just got in last night."

"And where's your better half?"

Jack must be Denton's boss, the man who was on his honeymoon, Elle realized.

"Rachel will be down in a minute."

Denton turned toward her. "Jack is CEO of Eyes. He founded the company several years ago."

"And brought along the best men with me. Men like Denton."

"Everyone's just trying to make me blush today."

Denton seemed way too masculine to actually blush. But his sense of humor made him less intimidating and more approachable.

Why did he have to be so approachable?

Elle frowned. She was really going to have to keep up her guard around Denton in order to keep her heart safe.

Arm's length. Why was arm's length getting harder and harder?

Denton left Elle in Rachel's capable hands so he could go up to his office and do some research. He'd been able to get the video feeds from the gala last night, but he needed better equipment in order to blow up the frames.

The deeper he got into this case, the less sense it made.

The fire inspector said his preliminary findings showed that a pipe bomb had been left in a janitor's closet. Denton's men had inspected that closet earlier, however. The bomb hadn't been there. So just how had someone managed to get through security with it?

He pulled up the video feed on his computer and watched the people on the screen. His feeling last night had been that something was off. Would these tapes help him to discover what?

He smiled when he saw he and Elle enter the ballroom. She'd looked gorgeous. Of course, she always looked gorgeous. But she'd had a special glow about her that night. At least, she had until her run-in with Preston.

Brianna had told him before the ball that Preston had proposed to Elle there last year. He couldn't believe the man had the nerve to show up and announce he was engaged again. Some people…

Denton squinted at an image on the screen. That's what was off.

He zoomed in on a picture. All of the security guards wore the same uniform. But one of them wore a shirt without pockets on the front. He printed the image. He had a feeling this was the man they were looking for.

Now he needed to figure out if Elle recognized him.

Elle paused from her conversation with Rachel and smiled as she watched the woman's six-year-old son battling with two plastic superhero toys. The three of them had spent the past couple hours getting to know each other in the living room of Rachel's home, a nice house situated at Eyes's headquarters.

Rachel, a stunning brunette who ran her own nonprofit to encourage members of the military, took a sip of her coffee and leaned back into the couch. "I'm sorry to hear about everything you're going through. I know it may not seem like it, but things will get better. You're in good hands with Denton."

Elle leaned back into her seat also, just for a moment feeling normal and relaxed—something she hadn't felt in nearly a week. "You sound like you speak from experience."

Rachel tucked her legs under her and shrugged, glancing once more at her son as he played on the rug. "I probably wouldn't be alive if it weren't for Jack and Denton. Believe me, I'd tell you the whole story but you probably wouldn't believe me. It was crazy—and terrifying. But here I am, alive and in love. Things have a way of working out for the best."

Elle traced the top of her coffee mug with her finger. "That's a good reminder because sometimes it doesn't feel like anything is going to work out."

A knock sounded at the door, and Denton stepped into the room. "How's it going, ladies?"

Elle sat up straighter at the sight of him. "Great. Rachel was just giving me some pointers on starting a nonprofit."

Rachel flashed a grin and set her coffee cup on the end table. "Elle has some really great ideas. I hope she's able to pursue them."

Denton sat down beside her, and Elle was instantly aware of his close proximity. His familiar cologne simultaneously soothed and electrified her. His leg grazed hers in a way that she was all too aware of. She knew what all of the signs meant. They meant that she was way too attracted to Denton for her own good. She tried to tamp down her feelings to no avail.

He held out a grainy black-and-white photo in front of her. "Do you recognize this man?"

Elle took the picture and studied it. Had she ever seen this man? Her first instinct was no. She looked closer. "He doesn't look familiar. Is this the man who planted the bomb? Is he a police officer?"

Denton shook his head. "No, he was dressed as a security guard, but his uniform is slightly different than the others. I feel pretty confident that he's our guy. Now we just have to figure out who he is."

"How are you going to do that?"

"We'll run the photo through some databases and see if there are any matches."

"Maybe this is the evidence we need to put these guys behind bars."

"I hope so." Denton looked at the picture and shook his head. "They're pretty clever. I'll give them that. Probably the only person who could have gotten an explosive through the front door was someone dressed as a security guard."

"We're dealing with two guys—three, if we count the driver—who are a lot smarter than I gave them credit for. Smart and deranged isn't a good combination," Elle said.

Denton grimaced. "You're right. It isn't."

Rachel stood. "Aiden and I are going to find Jack. Nice to meet you, Elle."

"Bye, guys." Elle's smile quickly faded as they closed the door behind them. She turned to Denton, feeling the strain across her back. "I still don't understand why they're targeting me. Because of the bank robbery? It just doesn't make sense. I didn't see them. I can't identify them, so I shouldn't be a threat."

"I think there's more to it than that, Elle."

She bristled. "What do you mean?"

"I think you were the target of that bank robbery. I think someone is playing a terrible game and that bank robbery was just to throw us all off."

Elle's heart thudded, resounding all the way down to the depths of her soul. What if what he said was true? She licked her lips. "*Terrible* is an understatement. Three people are dead and eleven people were injured at the gala. Who would do something like that?"

"Someone sick, twisted, with a vendetta against you. Remember, we only have a potential picture of one of the men. There's another one who's still faceless. Maybe you would recognize him. Is there anyone who has a reason to be upset with you, Elle?"

"My father works in politics. Before that he was a judge and a trial lawyer. There are a lot of people with a lot of reasons to be upset with my dad and, by association, me."

"Anyone who stands out?"

She exhaled slowly. "The man who kidnapped my sister was angry at my father. Of course, he's in jail now."

"He could have someone on the outside, some psycho who looks up to him and wants to finish his work."

Elle shuddered. "You think?"

"We have to explore every option." Denton's eyes looked serious. "Can you tell me about your sister's murder, Elle?"

"What do you want to know?"

"Tell me about the man who was arrested."

"His name is Richard Clements. My father was presiding over a case where he was the defendant. While driving under the influence, he hit a man and crippled him. He had the nerve to blame the bar that let him leave while intoxicated. While he was out on bond, he disappeared. That's when my sister was snatched."

"How long did he have her?"

"A week."

"Did he send a ransom letter?"

"He did, but the FBI advised us not to pay the ransom." She glanced at her fingers. "I've been told that even if we had paid the ransom, she probably would have died anyway."

Denton reached over and squeezed her hand. "I'm sorry, Elle."

"Me, too." She shook her head, deep in thought. "They could have killed me already. They've had the opportunity. At the bank. Even at the gala. They could have just shot me. But they didn't."

A thought slammed into her mind, and she flinched. One of the threats against her had read "Agony awaits." A clear picture began to form as realizations settled in her mind.

Denton's hand covered her knee. His eyes looked concerned as wrinkles formed in their corners. "What is it, Elle?"

She swallowed so hard that it hurt. "The note I found at the debate said 'Agony awaits.' I just realized that these guys want to cause me as much pain as possible, don't they? This is all on purpose, all a means of ratcheting up my anxiety, trying to paralyze me with fear. And it's all leading up to the moment where it's my turn." The color drained from her face at the mere thought.

Denton squeezed her knee again. "I'm not going to let that happen, Elle."

Elle nodded. The even bigger question was: How many people would be hurt or killed before these men got to her? And could she live with herself, knowing that the path of destruction was caused on the killers' way to her?

She closed her eyes. Agony—yes, agony—seemed to fill her.

These madmen were getting their way.

Lord, what am I supposed to do?

ELEVEN

As Denton and Elle headed down the road, Elle already missed the security that being at Eyes's headquarters had provided. For a brief moment while there, she'd stopped looking over her shoulder and questioning everyone's motives. She'd almost let herself forget about the trouble at hand.

Except that she would never really forget. It was always there, nagging her, causing her muscles to tense.

Could this be connected in some way to Emily's death?

Denton had sent the picture over to the FBI's Norfolk field office. Maybe they would have some answers for them before too long. The strain of living this way was beginning to get to her.

Maybe this was the time she should take a vacation to the Caribbean. Except—would she even be safe there? Was she safe anywhere?

As they rolled past the woods surrounding the road, Elle glanced down at her cell phone to see if Brianna had called her back yet. Nothing. Strange. It was unlike her friend not to get back with her.

"What's wrong?"

She held up her cell phone. "I've been trying to get a hold of Brianna, but I haven't heard from her all day."

"Is that unusual?"

"She keeps that cell phone close like some women keep jewelry close." Elle shook her head. "She's going through a nasty divorce, and her emotions get the best of her sometimes. And I have a tendency to worry too much."

"Did you try her landline?"

"She doesn't have one. Just a cell."

"Do you want to swing by her place and check on her?"

Her heart lifted. Just one visit and her fears could be alleviated. "Could we?"

"Sure. Just tell me where to go."

Elle gave him directions and they detoured from the route back to Elle's parents' house. Her gaze roamed her surroundings, but nothing appeared out of place. What did she expect to see—men with guns on every corner? People dressed in black dodging behind signs? She shook her head, chiding herself. But, even with her doubt, she remained on edge.

She had to remain on edge for her safety. All it would take was one moment of letting her guard down and her life could be changed forever.

"How long have you and Brianna known each other?" Denton asked.

"Since high school. We went our separate ways in college but then reconnected afterward. She was into doing pageants and has more crowns and titles than I can count. We actually competed against each other for Miss Virginia."

"And when you won, did it affect your friendship?"

Elle shook her head. "No, not all. Brianna's a good friend. I'm sorry she's been going through this divorce. It's been really hard on her. Her ex…well, I guess he wasn't ready to get married. That was no excuse, however, for being unfaithful."

"So in the midst of their divorce, you hired her as your assistant?"

"She needed a job. I needed an assistant. So yes, I hired her. It's been good for her to keep busy. As hurt as I was when

Preston and I broke up, I'm glad I discovered his indiscretions before we were married."

"Some guys give men a bad name."

"A lot of guys." She pointed to a road in the distance. "Turn here."

A moment later, they stopped in front of her friend's condo. Elle pointed to a red sedan in the distance. "Her car's here."

They walked to her door and rang the bell. After several minutes of silence, no one answered. Elle shook her head.

Denton turned to her, his hands on his hips. "Maybe she went out with someone who picked her up—and her cell phone is dead?"

Elle pulled out her keys. "Maybe. I'm going to check on things, just to make sure she's not lying in bed, too depressed to get up."

Denton wedged himself between her and the door. His closeness caused Elle to draw in a deep breath. She forced her eyes up to meet his, afraid that he might hear her stammering heart.

"I'll go first," he murmured.

His implications slammed into her heart, causing her to take a step back as horrid images filled her head. "You don't think…"

"I'm not assuming anything, but I'm not letting down my guard, either." Denton took the key from her and unlocked the door. He pushed open the door and quiet greeted them.

"Hello? Anyone home?" Denton called.

"Brianna, it's Elle. I'm coming in. Denton is with me."

"Stay behind me," Denton whispered, his gun drawn.

They crept into the house. Elle kept her eyes open for anything suspicious or out of the ordinary. Her friend had never been much of a housekeeper and today was no different. Piles of stuff were stacked everywhere. But nothing that hinted danger or trouble.

She's on a walk, Elle told herself. Just on a walk. Maybe she dropped her cell phone and broke it, and Elle would talk to her tomorrow and discover how all of this was a huge misunderstanding. They'd have a big laugh over everything.

So why did her stomach still clench with anxiety?

"Brianna, are you home?" Denton stepped over a clothes basket as they walked.

Still no response.

Denton nodded toward the hallway. Elle stayed behind him as they edged toward the bedroom doors. Denton threw open the first door. The spare bedroom waited on the other side. Everything appeared untouched and in place.

He stepped across the hall and opened the door to her bedroom. Again, nothing.

Elle didn't know whether to feel relief or fear.

Denton checked the rest of the house and the closets, but nothing seemed out of the ordinary.

A walk. Her friend had simply taken a walk. That's all there was to it.

Denton put his gun into his shoulder holster as they walked into her living room. "Do you want to wait for a few minutes to see if she comes back?"

Elle nodded, relief washing through her. "Just a few minutes. I think everything that's been happening lately is making me think the worst."

Denton didn't say anything. Probably because he didn't want to lie to her, which Elle appreciated. He knew just as well as Elle did that anything was possible and that no one was out of reach for these guys.

Elle paced from her friend's kitchen to the living room, trying to pass the time. She prayed as she walked.

Lord, protect my friend. Please. Let her be okay.

Just as she plopped on the couch, the doorknob rattled. Someone was trying to get in. Brianna? Or someone else?

Elle stood, wiping her sweaty hands on her jeans. Whoever was on the other side would either ease her fears or ignite them. She prayed for the prior.

How silly that she even had to think like this. A month ago, all of this would have seemed so paranoid. Her biggest concern might be that her friend met someone on her walk and was jumping into a relationship too soon.

Denton drew his gun again, and held out his hand to stop her. "Wait there."

Elle nodded and watched as Denton crept toward the door. Before he reached it, the door swung wide. A man stood on the other side.

"Identify yourself." Denton raised his gun.

The man—a stocky blond—threw his hands in the air and stepped back. "Whoa. Who are you? Where's Brianna?"

Elle stepped from the other room, her eyebrows scrunched together in concern. "Alex? What are you doing here?"

The man's hands remained raised in the air. "I was talking to Brianna on the phone when the line went dead. We were supposed to meet for lunch to talk but she never showed. I thought she was just being a jerk, so I decided to stop by her place to remind her that my time is just as valuable as hers."

Elle crossed her arms over her chest, obviously aggravated with the man's arrogance. "She's not here, and she hasn't been answering her phone. Did she say she was going anywhere else?"

Alex shook his head, beads of sweat sprinkling across his forehead. "No. Not that I asked." He looked at Denton and tilted his head. "Could you put that gun down?"

Elle stepped closer and put her hand on Denton's arm. "This is Brianna's soon-to-be ex. He's…harmless."

Denton lowered his gun, wondering if "harmless" was

Elle's first choice to describe the man. "Do you always just let yourself in?"

He shifted as if caught in a lie. "Old habits are hard to break. This used to be my place, too, you know." His gaze wavered between them. "What's going on? Why are you two here?"

Elle wrapped her arms over her chest. "We're worried about Brianna. We were just waiting around a few minutes to see if she returned."

"I would like to speak to her when she returns, also."

"Then please, have a seat and wait with us."

Alex stomped over to the couch, looking put off by Denton's take-charge attitude. Denton didn't care. The only thing he cared about was keeping Elle safe—and keeping everyone around Elle safe. With each passing moment, that task was becoming more and more difficult.

He paced the room, biding his time until Brianna returned. Elle stood near the kitchen door, her face pale—too pale. If he didn't have the self-control he'd learned over the years, he'd march over to her and pull her into a hug. But he couldn't. Elle was his assignment, and protecting her was the only thing on his to-do list. Falling in love wasn't an option, professionally or emotionally. The more he got to know Elle, the harder that restriction became, though.

Something beeped. Elle's hand went to her pocket, and she pulled out her cell phone. She looked down at the screen, lines forming on her forehead. "I've got a text message."

Denton stepped closer, still not dropping his guard with Alex around. "Anything important?"

"It's from Brianna."

Denton stood behind her, reading over her shoulder. The words there confirmed his worst fears.

We've got your friend. What are you willing to do to get her back?

Elle's hand flew over her mouth as if she tried to restrain her cry of despair. "Is this real? The men who are after me got Brianna, too?"

"Text them back. Say you need to speak to Brianna."

Elle's hands trembled on the phone's keyboard. Finally, she hit Send. The minutes ticked by as they waited for a response. Come on. Would Brianna's captors let her talk to them? They had to.

Elle looked up at him, her eyes wide. "Why would they do this?"

"I don't have any answers for you yet, Elle."

"Are you saying that someone abducted Brianna?" Alex's face showed his disbelief. His entire body looked tight. His mouth didn't quite close. "What exactly is going on?"

"We're trying to figure that out. You need to keep your cool." Denton suspected that this man knew something he wasn't telling them. He wasn't sure what or if it tied in with Brianna's disappearance. He intended on finding out, though.

"Should I text them again?" Elle's voice rose in pitch until cracking. "What should I tell them I'll do? Anything to get Brianna back safely."

"No, you can't tell them that. It's the exact wrong thing to tell them. First, we need to talk to Brianna. They have to prove that they really have her and that she's unharmed."

"This is all my fault. Everything." Tears filled her eyes.

"That's ridiculous. Don't blame yourself for the actions of evil men. They're the only ones to blame."

She squeezed the bridge of her nose. "This is a nightmare."

He slipped an arm around her shoulders. "We'll get through this."

Alex stepped forward, fire in his eyes. "Your friendship with Brianna is why she was abducted?"

Denton took a step forward, feeling the need to shelter Elle from any more pain than she'd already endured. "Back off."

"We need to call the police." He began pacing.

"You're right. Why don't you call them on your cell? I don't want to tie up Elle's line, just in case." Denton turned toward Elle. "Text them again. Tell them you need an answer. Keep the ball in your court."

The trembles in Elle's fingers had worsened to the point that none of the words she typed were understandable. Denton eased the phone from her fingers and typed the message himself. Another five minutes passed with no response. In the background, they could hear Alex reporting Brianna's disappearance. Denton would have to get on the phone himself and tell all the proper authorities.

He put a hand on her shoulder. "The police will be here in a minute. We'll wait until they get here."

The strain in Elle's eyes was enough to break his heart. She quickly wiped under her eyes, obvious in her attempt to remain strong. Her trembling voice belied her fear, though. "Why aren't they responding? What does that mean?"

"It's hard to say."

"Oh, Denton." She let a sob escape.

Against his sensibilities, Denton pulled her into his arms. It felt natural, as if they'd done it a million times before. Her sweet fragrance filled his senses, bringing him a temporary measure of peace. Only momentary, though. There were too many things to worry about for him to enjoy Elle's company too much.

He pulled back, using every ounce of strength within himself to let go of Elle. "I need to make a few phone calls while we wait."

Elle nodded, pain staining her gaze. She stared vacantly in the distance, her eyes red and rimmed with tears.

As soon as Denton pulled out his cell phone, Elle's began playing a cheerful melody that contradicted the somber mood of the house. Her eyes widened as she looked at the screen. "It's Brianna."

He stepped closer. "Stay calm and answer. Listen carefully to any signs as to where she is."

Elle nodded and put the phone to her ear. Denton leaned in close so he could hear. "Brianna, is that you?"

"Elle. You've got to help me." Brianna's voice teetered on the edge of panic. Every other syllable seemed to break with tension.

"I want to help you. Are you okay?" Elle's voice broke. Her entire body looked tight with strain. "Where are you?"

"I don't know, Elle. I don't know where I am. It's so dark and cold." Brianna let out another sob. The sound was gut-wrenching, laced with pulse-pounding fear.

A masculine voice in the background growled, "That's enough!"

"Wait!" Elle screamed.

A scraggily voice came on the line. "Think about what you'll do to get her back. Think long and hard because you don't want this case to end like your sister's."

The line went dead.

Elle looked up at Denton, her face drained of any color.

Then she erupted in sobs.

TWELVE

Elle paced in front of the windows of her bedroom, absently biting her fingernails. Usually work was her drug, her escape from all her other problems. But even keeping herself busy with work didn't help today. All she could think about was Brianna.

And Emily.

Panic squeezed her insides. Not again. How could something like this happen twice in her life? First, her sister, who'd also been her best friend. And now her best friend, who was like a sister to her.

The authorities were all working on the case. In fact, the FBI, along with local police, had set up a command post downstairs in their living room, complete with computers and other equipment that Elle couldn't identify. Denton was with them right now, pacing with his sleeves rolled to his elbows, looking every bit the part of a high-powered official.

Elle pictured all of them. They were probably plotting and theorizing and strategizing, she supposed. It didn't matter. All that mattered was finding Brianna. But with each minute that passed, Elle found her hope deflating.

She'd held on to hope that Emily would be found and brought back home. Hope had kept her going for those first few days. It had been like the air she breathed. But then the days continued to pass with no word. The press had a field day with the story, but Elle didn't even care—not if all their reporting managed to somehow help them get Emily back.

But nothing had helped. Despite all the negotiating and searching, the kidnapper had known from the start how everything would end. He'd known he would kill Emily.

And with that, Elle's life had been changed forever. She was now an only child whose already overprotective parents were sure to be even more sheltering. Some of the light and the life in their little family had disappeared.

For weeks, everyone walked around seeming like an empty shell. Elle had tried to put on a good front, to be the strong one, at least in front of her parents. But inside her heart was broken.

Her grandmother was the only one who'd really reached out to her. Sure, Elle had seen counselors and people had looked at her with pity in their eyes. But only her grandmother had seen through everything and realized how devastated Elle truly was.

And now her grandmother was gone, too.

Did everyone she loved have to die?

A knock tapped at the door. Elle pivoted toward the sound, staring at the wood a moment. Who could it be? Did they come bearing more bad news? "Come in."

Denton stepped inside, looking just the way she remembered seeing him earlier. Strikingly handsome. Strong but gentle, as he'd evidenced in the brief moments of comfort he'd offered. But still, no matter how Elle looked at it, he was someone who liked to live on the edge. He was off-limits.

Arm's length, she reminded herself.

Denton stepped closer, his five o'clock shadow a little darker than usual today. Even his presence in her room seemed to cause electricity to crackle through the air, seemed to heighten all of Elle's senses. She swallowed her emotions and dared to meet his eyes.

"How's it going?" His gaze was firm but inquisitive and compassionate.

She shrugged and drew her arms tighter around herself. "You tell me. Any news?"

He stared at her a moment, his hand twitching as if he contemplated reaching out for her. Finally, he nodded. "They've got some video feed from the parking lot. It's the same man from the gala. He was parked beside Brianna's car and apparently asked her a question or initiated some kind of conversation. She stepped closer to the man's van when someone pulled her inside."

Elle squeezed her eyes closed. "Have they made any more contact?"

"No, nothing."

"They're probably waiting on me." Waiting on Elle. She was the common denominator here. Yet she felt powerless to do anything.

Brianna's voice replayed in her mind, and Elle could hear her friend's desperation and fear. What were they doing to her sweet friend? Tears threatened to squeeze out.

Denton appeared at her side. His hands grasped her arms. "They're playing a game with you, Elle. A sick, twisted game."

"And the next step of the game could be the death of my best friend." Powerless. But did she have to be? There had to be something she could do. She opened her eyes, feeling a new resolve build in her. "Do you have any suspects? Did the photo match any in the system?"

Denton shook his head. "No matches."

Who else could it be? Who were the main suspects in her mind? Her thoughts immediately went to Emily's disappearance and murder. "Did you check the visitor record for the man who killed my sister?"

Denton slipped his hands from her arms and took a step back, snapping back into professional bodyguard mode. "He hasn't had any visitors in a year. We're still looking into him, though, checking any other records or things that might give us a clue if he's been corresponding with someone."

If this wasn't connected to her sister, then who? Who were those other suspects that constantly saturated her thoughts? "How about a member of my dad's staff? Is that still a possibility?"

"Anything is possible. There's obviously an accomplice, and we have no idea what he looks like. He could be anyone."

She paced over to the window, shaking her head as she shoved aside a curtain and stared at the barrage of cars parked out front—cars belonging to her family, Eyes, the FBI. What a nightmare. Everything that had happened just didn't seem real. "This was never about the bank robbery. That's what floors me. Whoever is behind all of this had some kind of master plan this whole time, didn't they? And everything has fallen in place for them. They've had us on wild goose chases, searching up and down. But the whole time, they had an end goal. Me."

She didn't have to look over her shoulder to know that Denton was beside her again. She could feel his presence igniting every fiber of her being.

"There are sick people in the world, Elle. I've looked into the eyes of men who didn't seem to have a soul. It chills you down to the core."

She looked up at him, his words causing cold fear to race through her veins. "You've seen your share of evil."

"Unfortunately."

"How do you keep your sanity?"

"By focusing on the eternal. Remembering that this world isn't our real home."

She nodded, processing his words. "Good perspective. I like that. I guess I haven't been spending as much time keeping my thoughts focused lately. I've let life consume me."

"It's easy to do."

"I want to help. I want to do something before someone else is hurt…or worse."

"Let the FBI handle it."

"That's what everyone told us with Emily." She shook her head. "I want to see the picture of the security guard at the gala again. Something's nagging me about it, but I don't know what."

His gaze stayed on her a moment too long before he finally nodded. "Okay. Let's go downstairs."

With a hand on her back, he led her downstairs and into what used to be her living room. The place had been transformed. All nonessential staff, volunteers and interns had been cleared out until this was over and in their place were FBI agents. Bentley sat at a nearby table, his face pale as if he hadn't gotten any sleep—probably because he hadn't. No one had, not since Brianna disappeared.

It seemed like everyone stopped what they were doing when Elle stepped into the room. She forced a courtesy smile and kept her mission forefront in her mind. Look at the picture. Figure out what was bugging her. She could do this. She could face everyone, even if they blamed her for her friend's disappearance just like Alex did.

Denton took a picture from the table and handed it to her. "Did you remember something?"

She shook her head. "Not yet. I'm hoping I will." She looked at the picture again. Why did he look familiar to her? Where had she seen this man?

"Could you guys take away his hat and give him a buzz cut or something a little shorter?"

An FBI agent sat down at a laptop computer and started tapping the keys. A moment later, an altered picture of the man appeared.

"Can you make his face thinner?"

An updated picture popped on the screen.

Denton leaned toward the computer from behind her. "Do you recognize him?"

"I think that man used to work IT for my father." She searched her memory for a clearer image of the man. All she could remember was the way he'd watched her. He hadn't struck her as too unusual at the time, simply socially inept. "Up in Dad's D.C. office. I remember he always gave me the creeps. I always felt like he was watching me. He was thinner when I remembered him and his hair was shorter, lighter."

"Do you remember his name?"

She shook her head. "No, I have no idea. I don't know if I ever knew." She looked over at Bentley, who hung out to the side. "Bentley, can you find the name of the company we used?"

The man nodded and immediately left the room to head toward the office.

Elle's heart pounded erratically. Could this be the clue they'd been looking for? She prayed the answer was yes.

Denton squeezed her shoulder. "Good job, Elle. Good job."

Elle downed another cup of coffee, trying to pass the time and ward away her feeling of helplessness. She sat in an armchair in the corner of her living room, listening to the flurry of activity and theories being thrown out all around her. Her mind turned over her encounter with the man from the photo. She prayed that she might remember something else—anything else—that would help the authorities find the man.

"You know the caffeine is only going to make you more jittery." Denton raised an eyebrow at her as he lowered himself into the seat near her.

"Is it possible to be more jittery than I already am?" She shook her head. "Time is of the essence when someone is missing. Each second that goes by makes me feel like Brianna's never coming back."

"They found the name of the IT company. Now they're just trying to identify the man. We're getting closer, Elle."

But would they get closer fast enough? She shoved down the thought, trying to stay positive.

"Something else interesting about the IT company…Bob Allen uses the same company."

Elle sat up straighter. "As in the Bob Allen who's running against my father?"

"The one and only."

"He couldn't be involved in this…could he?"

A knock sounded at the door, and one of the agents strode over to answer. Alex stood on the other side, looking as bad as Elle had ever seen him with his clothes and hair rumpled and circles under his eyes. Elle motioned to let him come in and then rose to meet him.

"Are there any updates?"

Elle shook her head. "No. None."

"How could this happen?"

Denton stepped closer. "What do you know that you're not telling us?"

Alex visibly tensed. "What do you mean?"

"There's something you're not saying. I want to know what it is. Why did you really go to Brianna's apartment today?"

He raised his hands. "I have nothing to do with this."

Elle remembered the suspicious way he'd acted. "You didn't just show up with plans to casually let yourself in, did you?"

He ran a hand through his hair. "Look, I came over to convince her to give my grandmother's wedding ring back. It's special to my family, and Brianna was being stubborn in keeping it, just doing it to hurt me. That was it—the only reason I stopped by. Nothing else."

Across the room, one of the agents stood. "We've got another text message."

"Put a trace on the phone, see if we can determine where it's coming from," another agent said.

A flurry of agents crowded around the phone. Elle stood, took a step closer. She'd never get close to the phone. She knew that. Her heart pounded in her ears as she waited to hear what the message said.

"'Time is ticking away and with each tick the pain becomes greater. This is all for you, Ellebird,'" an agent read.

All the color drained from Elle's face. She took a step back and lowered herself into the chair behind her.

Denton knelt in front of her. "Ellebird?"

"My grandmother used to call me that."

"Who would know that?"

"Only someone who'd been around my family." She shook her head, trying to dislodge the thoughts there. "The pain becomes greater? What are they doing to my friend?"

"A picture just popped onto the screen," an agent said.

Elle started toward the phone when Denton stopped her. "I want to see—"

He shook his head, a certain somberness falling over him. "Let me look at it first."

"It's Brianna," Agent Duffield, the lead in the investigation, said.

Elle could hardly breathe as Denton stood and went to peer at the phone. He shook his head and looked over at her. Elle knew what that meant. It meant she couldn't see the picture, which meant Brianna... She couldn't let her thoughts go there. She couldn't let herself imagine what the picture might look like.

"Is she okay? How does she look?" she asked anyway.

"She's alive," Denton murmured.

"Oh, Brianna…" She covered her face with her hands, trying to erase the images that crept into her mind. Denton put his hand at her elbow as if he feared she might pass out.

"What can I do?" Alex shifted, looking ill at ease.

Denton shook his head. "Nothing. Go home. We'll call you if we need something."

He nodded, slowly, regretfully, as his eyes met Elle's. "I would never wish this on her, you know," Alex explained.

Elle sighed, a new somberness washing over her. "I know."

He turned and strode to the door. As soon as Alex had left, Denton turned to her. "Come on. Let's take a walk while they get things figured out. The fresh air will be good for you."

"Is it safe?"

"We'll stay close to the house."

They stepped outside and the sunny day greeted them like a much-welcomed hug. They walked several paces in silence, and Elle felt grateful for the change in environment. Maybe the fresh air really would do her some good.

Denton stuffed his hands into his pockets. "You said your grandmother died a year ago?"

Elle nodded. "That's right."

"How often did she call you Ellebird? All the time? Ever in public?"

"She called me that all the time. But she didn't often go out in public with us as a family. She didn't like the limelight." She glanced at him. "What's wrong? Why are you frowning?"

"Elle, if your grandmother died a year ago, I'm afraid these guys have been planning this for a long time. How else would they know that?"

"You think they were around my family just for the purpose of one day doing this?"

He nodded. "I do. Was the IT guy ever at your house?"

She shook her head. "No, I only saw him up at my dad's D.C. office." She paused. "Now that I think about it, he may have been at the campaign office in Norfolk, also. He was from an outside firm that we used whenever we had computer problems."

"That would explain how someone hacked into your father's email account and website so easily."

She shivered. "They've been planning this a year. That's disturbing, to say the least. And they chose to implement their little plan right now while my father is trying to get reelected. That's probably not a coincidence."

"The FBI is on it. They'll figure out who this guy is. And maybe then we'll be able to track him down, figure out who his partner is, also."

Elle nodded, not wanting to admit that her hope was dying little by little.

She had to find a way to keep it alive, though. She had to find a way to keep Brianna alive.

Another wave of insomnia kept Elle unsettled, praying for sleep to find her. She had too much on her mind to sleep. Too many worries. Too many fears.

She simply couldn't get Brianna out of her mind. Every time she closed her eyes, she pictured what her friend might be going through. The sheets lay twisted at her feet, evidence of her anguish. Finally, she sat up and threw her feet over the edge of the bed. Her heart raced and her throat felt dry with emotion as she stared at the dark room around her. The only light was that of the moon outside that shone in through her window.

She raked a hand through her hair. She'd tried desperately to come up with a plan to appease Brianna's abductors. If she could get her phone, maybe she could text them, let them know she'd trade herself for Brianna. Those around her would never let that happen. There were eyes on her all the time, especially Denton's.

Denton.

He'd been such a support to her during this crazy experience.

Of course he had been. He'd been hired to protect her. Somehow, she'd begun feeling like he was more than hired help, though. He felt like a friend, maybe even like... She swallowed. No, she couldn't think like that. She needed someone safe, predictable. Someone who valued routine and stability and privacy. Not someone who took chances for a living. When would she ever learn her lesson?

Finally, she stood, stretching as she did so. She would give in to her insomnia. Maybe she could at least read a book and drink some milk, do something that might get her mind off everything going on and help sleep find her. She pulled on a robe over her pajama set and crept down the hallway. Denton's door remained closed. Maybe this would be the one time she'd be able to slip past him. The man seemed to have a sixth sense that clued him in whenever she tried to do something without his knowledge.

She tiptoed downstairs, shivering as she stepped onto the wooden floor. The house, at the moment, felt big and overwhelming. Not safe and secure. There were too many places for people to hide, too many shadows.

She knew there was an agent stationed outside, watching for anything suspicious. Certainly she was safe in her own house. All the campaign staff and law enforcement personnel had cleared out.

Tonight, it was just her, her mother, Denton and Bentley.

Her father was still in D.C. He had his own security detail with him.

What if her father was really the target in all this? What better way to get at her father than by getting to her? Because really there was no one she could think of who'd hate her this much. Preston would have the most reason to be upset with her—he'd tried to convince her for months that they should get back together. But now he was engaged. He'd obviously gotten over her. Besides, he was the one who had cheated.

But Preston would have known that her grandmother called her Ellebird. He knew the family's schedule. He knew Brianna was her best friend. Had he been the one who recommended that IT firm?

Tension pinched her back muscles.

No, Preston couldn't be behind this.

But she had to acknowledge that there was a chance it was someone her father knew and trusted or had hired.

If not Preston, then who?

Bentley? Denton seemed to think it was a possibility, but she had a hard time believing it. The man was set in his ways and determined, but he would never do this. He was too intent on her father being reelected.

Of course, her father's numbers had climbed since the press got wind of everything that had happened. Bentley wouldn't do this just to get votes…would he? She shook her head. No, he was conniving, but not that conniving. Still, doubt lingered.

She tried to think of someone—anyone—else, but her mind drew a blank. She liked to believe the best in people, but she truly couldn't think of anyone this evil or twisted. Not even Preston or Bentley.

As she stepped into the kitchen, resolve settled in her. She was going to look into the people who openly disliked her father. The ones who'd sent him death threats, posted nasty messages or organized protests.

She knew the FBI was investigating, and she trusted them. But right now she had to do something to help her friend and investigating on her own was all she could think of. Besides, her investigating would take place behind a computer desk. That seemed safe enough.

As she stepped toward the cabinet where the glasses were kept, she decided to keep the lights out. The illumination from the inside of the refrigerator should be enough to let her see what she was doing. She grabbed a glass and pulled out the milk.

As she closed the door, something at the window caught her eye. She squinted, caught in a moment of fight or flight.

She wanted to run, but her hand felt frozen on the refrigerator handle.

Finally, the discrepancy that caught her eye came into focus.

There, on the bay window by the breakfast nook, something had been smeared on the window. Something white. Letters. Words. A message.

A threat.

We're watching you.

She dropped her milk and screamed.

THIRTEEN

Denton had heard Elle slip out of her room. He'd quietly dressed, trying to give her space but wanting to be ready in case she needed him. He pictured her tiptoeing downstairs to get a midnight snack. But he could also picture her trying to sneak out and help her friend. That's why he had to be on guard.

A scream ripped through the air.

Denton grabbed his gun and raced out of his room. He took the stairs by twos, desperate to get to Elle, to find out what had happened, to make sure she was okay.

He halted in the kitchen doorway. Elle stood there, a pool of liquid and broken glass at her feet. Her face looked as pale as the milk on the floor.

She pointed to the window.

He read the words painted there, visible even in the dark. *We're watching you.*

How had those words gotten there? When? How had someone gotten past security outside the house?

He had to radio his agent and find out where he was. His gut told him something was wrong. No way had someone gotten this close to the residence with Agent Banks patrolling the premises.

He closed the space between him and Elle. "Are you okay?"

She grabbed some paper towels and began sopping up the mess on the floor. "Just surprised."

Denton knelt beside her and placed his hands over hers. "We'll get that in a moment. Right now, I need you to stay away from the windows, okay?"

She nodded. Denton raised her to her feet and led her to her mom's bedroom. "I've got to go check on my guy outside. I need you to stay here. Lock the door behind me, and don't answer for anyone but me. Understand?"

She nodded again, obviously shaken.

Denton waited until he heard the lock click in place before running downstairs. A sleepy-eyed Bentley stood in the foyer, a dazed look about him. "What's going on?"

"Stay inside with Elle and Mrs. Philips, and call me if you need me. I've got to go outside and check things out."

"I heard a scream. Is someone hurt?"

"Not on my watch."

Denton slipped outside, his gaze darting around for Agent Banks. He pulled out his cell phone and dialed his number. "Banks, you there?"

Nothing.

What had happened to his agent? Tension clinched his gut. "Banks?"

Still nothing.

Denton scanned the landscape, looking for a sign of trouble or a sign of life. Anything out of the ordinary that would give him a clue as to where to look.

In the distance, the door to the guard station stood ajar. He darted toward the small building. As soon as he got to the entrance, he drew his gun and stood on alert. He swung around the corner and took in the guard station.

Agent Banks lay on the floor, blood on his forehead. Quickly, he felt for a pulse. It was faint but there. He had to get him medical help and fast.

Just as he pulled out his phone, a noise caught his ear.

A beeping.

His eyes zeroed in on a blinking light in the corner.

A bomb.

And it was set to explode in five seconds.

Elle's mom pulled herself up in bed, strain obvious over her pulled features. Her cast weighed her down, made every movement harder.

"What's going on? I heard a scream."

Elle sat on the edge of her bed and flicked on a bedside lamp. "Someone left a message on the window downstairs. It said, 'We're watching you.'"

Her mother's eyes closed and a somber expression ingrained every part of her being. "Elle, I don't understand why all this is happening. Where's Denton?"

"He went to check things out on the property."

"Do you think this is all because of your father's indiscretions?"

Elle blinked. "You think it's because of the women he's rumored to have been with?"

"Could be. Someone may have finally decided to get revenge."

"They're going over-the-top with revenge, if that's the case. They're not even focusing on Dad. They're focusing on—"

"On you." Her mom nodded, her gaze heavy with grief. "Nothing makes sense."

"I'm hoping this will end soon. The country's best is working the case. I'm sure answers are close."

Her mom ran a hand over her face before raising her chin. She drew in a deep breath, composure replacing her exhaustion. "Thank goodness Denton is here. I don't think I would get any sleep at night without him."

"I agree." Denton did have a way of making people feel

safe. He was good at his job. "He's one of the country's best, too."

Elle hoped he was okay now, as well as Agent Banks. She'd expected him back by now—the silence and the waiting were enough to drive her batty. Just what was going on outside?

She got up and paced over to the window. She hoped the full moon might allow her to see something.

Nothing.

Only an expanse of lawn and the silhouette of trees at the edge of the property. The guard station stood at the end of the drive, surrounded by the iron fence. Elle bit her lip and stayed at the window a moment, hoping to catch a glimpse of Denton or Agent Banks. She just needed some sign that they were okay.

Just as she dropped the drape to return to her mother, an explosion lit the evening sky. She pressed her face to the glass and saw the guard station in flames.

"No!" Elle darted across the room toward the hallway.

Her mother lunged forward, trying to get up but unable to with her cast. "What's going on? What was that?"

Elle hurried toward the door, panic lacing each movement. "The guard station. It just went up in flames."

"Elle, come back here."

"No, I've got to make sure Denton is okay. I've got to call the police."

"I'll call the police. Elle—"

Elle didn't hear her mom. She flew toward the front door. Just as her hand covered the knob, strong arms grabbed her from behind.

"Where do you think you're going?"

She fought against the man's grasp. Her elbow came up and back and caught his eye. The man moaned and doubled over in pain. She flipped around, ready to fight. Then she straightened.

"Bentley?"

His hand covered his eye, but even then she could see his scowl. "I'm going to have a shiner, thanks to you."

She straightened from her fighting stance. "What are you doing grabbing me like that, especially after everything that's happened?"

He pursed his lips in aggravation. "Your little boyfriend told me not to let you go out there. I was just doing what he said."

"He's not my little boyfriend, and I need to see if he's okay." She reached for the door, but Bentley grabbed her arm again.

"You can't do that. It's dangerous. You don't know what's going on. Maybe the person who caused that explosion is waiting outside the front door. You've got to use your brain instead of your heart."

Elle paused, blood pounding in her ears. "You may be in charge of my father's staff, but you're not in charge of me." She pulled from his grasp and opened the front door. Her gaze scanned her surroundings a moment for any signs of danger.

Flames licked away at the building in the distance and the smoldering scent of smoke and ash fell heavy in the air. Before Bentley could reach for her again, she ran toward the explosion, ignoring any fears of what could happen or the situation she may have just put herself in.

She simply couldn't stay inside, sitting by idly, while someone may be outside and hurt. She knew if she'd stopped long enough to think about it, she would find this decision foolhardy. But sometimes emotions trumped logic.

Her bare feet pounded the prickly grass. Her mom should have called 9–1–1 by now. Hopefully emergency crews would be on their way.

Raging-hot debris littered the lawn. Elle slowed, stepping

carefully so as not to injure herself. She wouldn't be much help hurt.

"Denton! Agent Banks!" she called.

She saw no signs of life, only destruction. Her heart panged with grief. *Please, Lord, let there be no one inside of the building.*

She rounded the corner and spotted two bodies sprawled on the ground. Casualties of war? She prayed that wasn't the case.

Her heart froze as her eyes focused on the features of one of the men.

Denton.

She rushed toward him and knelt at his side. Blood gushed from his forehead. His shirt was stained red and ripped. He looked lifeless. She grabbed his arm and nudged him. "Denton?"

His eyes pulled open. Slowly, he raised up on his elbows. His hand went to his forehead before his gaze focused on her. "Elle. You shouldn't be out here."

"What happened? Are you okay?"

He grimaced with pain. "You should be inside."

"I couldn't stay inside, not when I thought you might be out here hurt." Her fingers reached for Agent Banks. She found his pulse. There, but barely. "He's still hanging on. Help is on the way. What happened?"

"Someone knocked Agent Banks unconscious and left a bomb. I got him out just in time."

Sirens wailed down the road. Help was on the way. Thank goodness help was finally on the way.

"Elle, I've got to get you back inside."

She shook her head. "No. Don't be ridiculous. I'm staying here with you."

"Elle…" His eyes implored her, weakening her resolve. But only for a moment.

"People have been sheltering me my entire life. Sometimes I have to follow my own instincts." She kept his head elevated in her lap. "Now you stay put until an ambulance gets here."

Despite his injuries, a smile curled part of his lip. "Yes, ma'am."

Maybe he'd be okay. Agent Banks, too. She had to believe that or she'd go crazy blaming herself. All of this was because of her. People around her kept getting hurt. How much longer could she go on, knowing that she was the key component to all these crimes?

"You're one stubborn lady, Elle Philips."

Elle smiled this time. "So I've been told." Her smile slipped. Eventually, she'd have to tap into that stubbornness in order to keep her family and friends safe. What other choice did she have?

Just then, the ambulance pulled to a stop outside the gate. Two EMTs ran over to help. Elle stepped back and let them do their job.

But as they bandaged up Denton and began to examine Agent Banks, a realization crashed into her mind. She cared about Denton. Too much.

She had to keep her distance. As hard as it was going to be, she had no other choice, not if she wanted to keep her heart safe. And if she wanted to keep him safe.

An hour later, Denton was bandaged and bruised, but no worse for wear. Agent Banks, on the other hand, had a concussion and had to be admitted to the hospital. The FBI was back again and investigated the explosion, as well as the threatening message.

Though it was the middle of the night, people milled about the house. Denton stood in the entryway of the home, his gaze focused on Bentley. His shoes in particular. There were wet grass blades on the bottom of his sneakers. Had Bentley been outside? Denton certainly hadn't seen him.

But someone had been outside to leave that message and to leave the bomb. Was Bentley capable of those things? Absolutely. But did he have a motive?

Denton wasn't sure.

"What are you thinking?" Elle appeared beside him.

"That you should have never gone outside."

"Besides that."

"Did Bentley go outside to help you?"

"No. Why?"

"He has grass on his shoes."

"You don't think…"

"I'm not ruling anyone out at this point. Bentley certainly has the inside track on what's going on in your life. It's entirely possible that he could be involved. Not likely, but possible."

Bentley turned away from the agent questioning him and stomped over to them at that moment. Fire lit his eyes. "I tried to keep her inside. I did. But she wouldn't listen."

Denton pointed at his feet. "You were outside."

He looked down and when he raised his head again, his cheeks flushed red. "I couldn't sleep. I just stepped onto the patio to have a drink."

"The patio doesn't have grass on it."

He frowned. "I paced around a little bit."

"A lot on your mind?"

"I'd say! Someone is trying to single-handedly destroy this campaign!"

Elle's hands went to her hips. "My dad's numbers have gone up. Are you sure this isn't helping his chances for re-election?"

"What are you suggesting? That I'm behind this? You're

crazy." He threw his hands in the air, his voice rising in pitch with every word.

Elle remained firm. "You had the day off when the bank robbery happened."

"I had a doctor's appointment. You can't think I'm the one who's killing people off! I can't believe you." He started to step away.

"I wouldn't go far. I'm sure the FBI will want to talk to you." Denton's voice cut through the air. Goose bumps popped over Bentley's arms, visible even from where Denton stood.

Bentley turned around, his nostrils flaring. "You're serious?"

Denton nodded. "Your defensiveness isn't helping your case, you know. It only makes you look guilty."

"I haven't done anything!"

Elle crossed her arms over her chest. "Then why do you look guilty?"

He raised his hands in the air. "Listen, I've let a few things leak to the media. That's it. I haven't been behind any of the crimes, though. I swear."

Elle's voice remained surprisingly steady. "Why would you let these things leak? Do you not value my family's privacy?"

"I value winning."

Elle's chin jutted out, and she stepped closer to her father's chief-of-staff. "I strongly suggest you not stay at our house anymore, Bentley."

Bentley blinked in obvious surprise. "Are you firing me?"

"That's up to my dad. I'm simply kicking you out of our house."

His face turned an explosive shade of red. "You'll regret this, Elle."

Denton pulled Elle back a step. "Is that a threat?"

He didn't respond. He turned on his heel and stormed away instead.

* * *

Elle sat at her desk, absently doodling and writing notes that didn't make sense, somehow trying to sort out her twisted thoughts. She began jotting down everything that had happened so far. Would this help? Probably not. But maybe getting all her thoughts out of her head and onto paper would somehow let her brain feel less cluttered.

Bank robbery.

Jimmy shot.

Email hacked.

Dad's D.C. neighbor stabbed.

Bombing during gala.

Brianna kidnapped.

Message on window.

Gatehouse bombed.

It just didn't make any sense. Elle wasn't a criminal justice major, but it just seemed like these guys were all over the place. Didn't most killers have a modus operandi—a certain way of doing things? The only link between these crimes seemed to be her family.

The FBI still hadn't been able to identify the man from the photo. He stopped working at the IT company six months ago, and his given identity was fraudulent. That basically meant he could be anyone. His accomplice was still faceless, and there was a possibility a third person was involved.

If one of those perps was somehow connected with the family, who could it be?

Bentley was the obvious choice at the moment. He knew about Elle's nickname.

But so did Preston.

Bob Allen had a reason to ruin her father's reputation. But would he sink that low?

Elle leaned her head back toward her chair, feeling the

start of a headache. She had to figure this out…for Brianna. For everyone she loved, for that matter.

She'd just spoken with Brianna's mom this morning, and the woman was a mess. She was booking a flight and heading out from California, where Brianna's family had moved two years ago. Alex had called several times and he seemed genuinely concerned.

"That paint on your window. It's the same stuff people use to write on car windows after weddings and football games." Denton strode into the room, proof of last night's blast still evident in the small scrapes across his face.

Elle's breathing quickened at the sight of him. Agent Banks was still in the hospital, but, last Elle had heard, would probably be released later today. Thank goodness no one had been hurt any worse.

She swiveled in her chair to face him. "Car window paint, huh? Who are the guys? Soccer dads who kill on the side?"

He sat down beside her and pointed at the paper. "What are you doing?"

She stared at her list and frowned. "Trying to make sense of things."

"Did it work?"

She shook her head. "Not in the least."

"What's going on with Bentley?"

"My dad's supposed to handle him. We'll see what happens."

"You think he's behind some of this stuff that's been going on?"

"It's hard to say. My gut says no. But who knows, really? I can't imagine anyone being this sick." She straightened. "Do you think it's odd that there seems to be no pattern to these crimes?"

He stared ahead solemnly for a moment before nodding. "I do. They have a method. We just don't know what it is yet."

She stared at the paper. "All these crimes…they just don't seem to fit."

He took the paper from her. "There's a link in there some-where. We just have to figure it out."

"My family. My family seems to be the only link."

"These men could be angry with your family for some reason. That's a definite possibility."

"But why go through all these different methods of crime? What sense does that make? Unless…"

"What is it?"

Elle's brain whirled as an idea ignited. She took the list back from Denton and scanned the crimes committed so far. She closed her eyes as her idea settled in her mind. Finally, she pulled open her eyes and set the list back on the table. "I need to call my dad."

"Elle, would you mind telling me what you're thinking?"

"Denton, I think someone is trying to make a statement by acting out some of the criminal cases my dad presided over as a judge or trial attorney."

He leaned forward. "Tell me more."

She pointed to the list. "I don't know about all of them. And this could be a stretch. But I know about some of the more high-profile cases because the media reported on them. One was a kidnapping of a girl from a parking lot. One was a bank robbery. Of course there were murders. I don't remem-ber the details of all of them, but I'd bet there was at least one shooting death and one stabbing."

"You could be on to something."

She shook her head. "The paint you said that they used on my window? One of my father's last cases was a college kid who was killed by a drunk driver after a football game. The car, which went up in flames, had messages written all over the windows." She paused and looked at Denton. "Am I crazy?"

He stood and shook his head. "No, I think you're brilliant."

FOURTEEN

"We've got a hit on a cell phone location."

Elle jumped from her seat and darted to the table where a cluster of federal agents had gathered. "Where? Can you get your guys out there?"

"Brianna's cell phone just came on out of the blue," Agent Duffield said. "It remained on for just long enough for us to get a location."

Denton's hands went to his hips. "Something smells fishy. Why would the cell phone just come on?"

Elle's heart surged with hope. "Maybe Brianna got it and turned it on."

Denton held out a hand to calm her. "Don't get your hopes up. These guys are conniving."

Agent Duffield sat back from the computer and tapped on his lips with a pen. "The location is only about ten miles from here. It looks like it's at an abandoned warehouse out in the Pungo area."

"What are you thinking?" Denton asked.

Agent Duffield stood and looked at the crowd of people waiting for his response. "Let's get some men out there. But we've got to be careful. This could be a setup."

"Or it could be a legitimate lead!" Excitement seemed to squeeze the air out of Elle's throat.

"I assure you that we realize that." Agent Duffield stepped toward the front door.

Elle stepped after him. "I want to go! I need to be there for Brianna, in case you find her."

Denton's hand gripped her arm, jerking her to a halt before she was carried out the door with the flood of agents who exited. "That's not a good idea. We need you here. Safe."

She looked up at Denton, the one person she'd come to trust throughout the whole fiasco. He was capable, smart and tough. "Are you going? Are you going to help them?"

He shook his head. "No, I need to stay with you."

"Why? They need you. Can't you—?"

"Elle, I'm not taking that risk in case this is a setup. Maybe they want us to leave you alone so they can swoop in here and act out yet another part of their grand plan. The FBI will do their job there." His gaze felt warm on hers as he lowered his voice. "My job is to protect you."

"Denton, I'm scared for her."

His hand traveled down her arm until he gripped her hand. "I know."

A figure filled the doorway. Elle gasped and stepped back from Denton. She looked over and spotted her father standing there, his brows drawn together. He wore his typical crisp business suit and had two advisors on either side of him. "What's going on?"

Denton's hand left hers, and Elle brought her arms over her chest. "The FBI thinks they know where Brianna is." Elle filled him in on the details.

"We can only hope for the best." He pulled off his overcoat. "This has gone on for a long time. Too long. Brianna's a nice girl. She doesn't deserve this. No one does."

"What are you doing home?"

"I couldn't stay in Washington, not with everything going on. There are some things more important than politics, just don't tell that to any of my supporters." He planted a kiss on her forehead. "How is your mother?"

Maybe her father was turning over a new leaf, so to speak. Could that be the one good thing to come out of this dreadful situation? Would her father realize how he had neglected his family? "She's sitting in the sunroom resting. Still recovering from the excitement of last night."

Her father shook his head and started toward the back of the house. "*Excitement* is putting it mildly. When's all of this going to calm down?"

"When we have these guys behind bars, is my guess." Denton shifted. "I have some questions for you, Senator Philips. Do you have a moment?"

Elle laid a hand on her father's arm. "Before that, I have to ask—did you meet with Bentley?"

"I did. I don't think the man is guilty, but I fired him anyway."

"Why?"

"I can't have someone on my staff who I don't trust and, right now, I don't trust him."

"Do I need to put together a press release?"

"It's not a bad idea. Better we do it first before Bentley takes matters into his own hands. He didn't take being let go very well."

"I can imagine."

Denton stepped forward. "I'd like Elle to be there when I talk with you about a new theory. Can we do that first?"

"Of course. Let's go to my office." Senator Philips pointed. "This way."

Her dad sat behind his massive desk and laced his fingers in front of him. Elle and Denton sat in the stiff leather chairs across from him.

Denton didn't waste any time. "We need to talk to you

about some of the trials you resided over as judge or worked as an attorney."

Her dad settled back into his desk chair. "What's this about?"

Elle and Denton exchanged a glance. Elle finally spoke up. "We think someone might be attacking people in a way that reflects different cases you were a part of."

Her father's eyebrows came together. "Why would someone do that?"

Elle shrugged. "Why do evil people do anything that they do?"

The door opened, and a member of housekeeping stood frozen in the doorway. The man backed away. "Sorry. I didn't realize anyone was here."

Elle waved him off, trying to ease his obvious anxiety. "No problem. But, please, work on the upstairs for now."

He nodded toward the distance. "Is it okay if I clean the message from the kitchen window?"

"The police have released that scene, so that should be fine," Denton said.

The man paused. "It may not be my place to say this, but I wanted to let you know that I saw a man creeping along the fence outside a few days ago."

"A man? What did he look like?" Denton asked.

"In his twenties. Red hair. Skinny as skinny could be."

Elle's gaze locked on her father's. "That sounds just like Travis Ambler!" She turned toward Denton. "He's the man who's made threats against my father in the past. He sits outside his office as a one-man protest sometimes. Something just doesn't seem right about the man. His animosity extends beyond the normal anger people have against politicians. Then the next moment he acts like he idolizes my dad."

Denton shook his head. "We had Ambler checked out."

"And?"

Denton sucked in a deep breath. "And he's accounted for during the bank robbery. In fact, a dozen people saw him sitting outside your father's campaign office in Norfolk."

Elle wasn't ready to let this drop. "Maybe there are more than two people involved. Maybe there are three. If he was creeping along outside the house, he could be our guy. Maybe there's some kind of twisted reasoning here that will help this to make sense."

Denton patted his hands in the air. "I'll make sure someone looks into it. I promise." His gaze turned back to her father. "Now, can we talk to you about some of those cases?"

"How about you tell me what you're thinking?"

Denton shifted in his seat. "A bank robbery?"

"I judged a case where a bank robber killed one of the tellers." Her father's face went still. Finally, he said, "Go on."

Elle cleared her throat. "The case where that college kid was killed by a drunk driver?"

"Right. I was the lawyer for the family whose son died. The drunk driver got five years after the car he hit exploded into flames."

"Just like the guardhouse," Elle mumbled. "What other high-profile cases were you involved with?"

"Probably the one that was the biggest media storm involved the girl who died in the undercover drug sting. She walked into the middle of the operation, and that drug lord they'd been trying to take down for years shot her before getting away. There were two police officers involved, but the accused was able to walk on a technicality—the authorities forgot to read him his Miranda rights. Later, the man went to jail on other charges, but never for this woman's murder."

Elle looked at Denton. "What could they be planning with that?"

Denton grimaced. "I don't know. It doesn't tie in with anything so far."

Elle's heart thudded with sorrow. "And then there's Brianna...."

The lines on her father's face tightened. "There was one kidnapping case I was involved with."

Elle leaned forward. "What happened?"

"The girl was snatched from outside a grocery store." He shook his head. "But she was found the next day."

"Found?"

"Dead."

Elle hung her head. "Brianna's been missing for a day. And she was snatched in a parking lot outside her apartment. Of course, these guys aren't following the cases detail by detail." Elle shivered. That didn't mean her friend would be killed today. It couldn't mean that. She had to keep hope alive.

Denton nodded. "Just enough to get their point across."

Her dad cleared his throat, a new somberness falling over him. "The only other kidnapping was..."

"Emily." Elle's nerves panged with tension.

Denton shifted in his seat to face Elle. "How long did they have Emily?"

"A week." Her throat burned as she said the words. Would the pain ever subside?

Denton touched the arm of her chair. She was certain he would have touched her had her father not been there. "How did they find her, Elle?"

"She was in the woods by a creek. She'd been dead for several days before they found her." What if there was a clue there? Or what if that's where they were holding Brianna? "I want to go there."

Denton shook his head. "Elle, that's not a good idea. I'll go."

"You can't go by yourself. You'll never find it."

Her dad stood. "You know where it is?"

"I go there all the time." She shrugged, realizing her admission. "I know it seems weird, but it just helps me to deal with everything that happened. I want to go. I'll show you."

Her father waved. "I'll call the police and let them know to meet you there."

Elle started toward the door. "Come on. Let's go." She didn't wait to see if Denton followed behind her as she darted toward the door leading to the garage.

"Whoa, Elle." Denton pulled her to a stop. "We've got to keep level heads here. I know you've got a lot of emotions right now. We can't let them get in the way of your safety."

Elle nodded. "I know. I just want to find her. I just want her to be okay."

"We're not going into the woods until backup arrives."

"Okay."

"Take a deep breath."

She sucked in air, trying to tamp down her emotions.

Finally, Denton nodded. "Okay, let's go."

As they bounced down the road, Denton couldn't help but think about worst case scenarios. His knuckles were white as he gripped the wheel. He had to keep Elle safe. The most important thing right now was ensuring that she wasn't hurt. Because that was what he'd been hired to do…and because he was starting to care about her.

Care about her in ways he shouldn't. Losing his wife had made him feel like his heart had been ripped out. He wasn't ready to love someone else again…or was he? Because Elle made his heart race like it hadn't raced in a long time. She filled his thoughts and made him look forward to each time they interacted. And when she cried, there was nothing more that he wanted than to pull her into his arms.

This wasn't good. Wasn't good at all.

He glanced over at her and saw her reaching for the empty

place at her throat where her necklace used to rest. That heirloom obviously meant a lot to her. "You doing okay?"

She nodded, but she didn't look okay. Her face was pale, her breathing heavy. "They're recreating a kidnapping. What kind of sick people are we dealing with?"

He rested his hand on her knee as they sped down the road. There was nothing he could say. They both understood the grave situation. Life hung in the balance. The two men had chosen to play God, to decide when someone's final day would be. Nothing seemed to stop the madmen, and all of their leads so far had gotten them nowhere. With every breath, danger loomed closer. Safety seemed a distant memory. Denton didn't remember feeling this level of uneasiness since his days in the Middle East as he faced insurgents who'd hated him simply because he was an American.

"Turn here," Elle directed. A few minutes later, they pulled to a stop at the edge of the woods. His cell phone rang as he put the SUV in Park. It was Elle's father.

"The police are on their way."

"Did they find anything from the cell phone trace?"

"Nothing."

"Thanks for the update. We just arrived."

Elle jumped out of the vehicle, and Denton scrambled around to her side. His gaze scanned the area for any signs of danger. Nothing. Not visible to the eye, at least.

"Come on." She started toward the tree line.

Denton grabbed her arm and pulled her back. "Not so fast, Elle."

"It's just right down that path." She took another step toward the trees.

"Elle, we need to wait for the FBI. We don't know what's waiting for us behind this parking lot."

"But what if Brianna…"

"I know." He pulled her into his arms, and she melted into

his embrace. He held her until he heard the sound of tires against the gravel. Then he righted himself, jumping back into professional mode.

Three police cars and an FBI sedan pulled to a stop. Once the team was assembled, Elle lead the officers down the path. Denton stayed at her side, his gaze roaming his surroundings for any sign of danger. Who knew what these guys were planning next?

The trail continued, deeper and deeper into the woodsy swampland. Elle didn't hesitate or cringe or show any fear. Her gaze only showed her determination and focus. The woman looked like she'd done this a million times before. Of course, she said she had been back here many times previous to today, all in honor of her sister. Denton could only imagine how painful those visits must have been, the memories that were sure to surface.

And now Brianna… How much grief could one heart take?

Finally, they stopped by a murky creek and followed the water along the banks. Their footing was rockier here as the trail gave away to the embankment.

"Not much farther," Elle called over her shoulder.

"Elle," Denton said.

She slowed, but only for a second.

"Let me go first."

"But—"

"Elle, let me go first. Just in case."

"In case what—?" Realization spread over her face. She paused and allowed him in front of her. "It's not much farther. Just a few feet."

He kept his gun raised, still unsure of what to expect.

But something ahead looked out of place. It looked like a white sheet had washed up…with something underneath it.

"Elle, wait here."

She halted, opened her mouth, but shut it just as quickly. Then she nodded.

Denton stepped forward. "Guys, keep an eye on her."

Agent Duffield and two other agents joined him.

They approached the sheet. Agent Duffield squatted down and moved the covering. Brianna's lifeless face stared back at them.

FIFTEEN

Elle's first impulse when they arrived back at the house was to shut down, to retreat to her room and mourn. The thought that she'd never see Brianna again, that they'd never be able to talk about men or fashion or lousy politics, seemed surreal.

Tears flooded her eyes as she slipped into her office, asking Denton for a moment alone.

How could someone be this cruel? Why so many innocent lives? And when would the insanity end?

She'd held on to the hope that things would get better, that these men would give up or be arrested. But neither of those things had happened. Instead, the danger was escalating, and more and more people were becoming victims.

Lord, why is this happening? Why would You allow such evil on earth?

Every part of her wanted to curl into a ball and sob.

But something clicked inside her.

She wouldn't let this stop her. She'd make sure Brianna's death strengthened her resolve to put an end to this madness. She'd use the loss of her friend to fuel the fight. She'd make sure her tears weren't wasted.

Her father strode into the room, pulling her into a hug. "I'm so sorry, sweetheart."

"I can't believe she's gone, Dad."

He stepped back, his expression more somber than she'd seen in a long time. Probably since Emily, for that matter. "I'm still trying to wrap my mind around everything. These men are cruel."

"Beyond cruel." She remembered her friend's lifeless expression and a sob caught in her throat. All the resolve in the world wouldn't lessen her pain, her loss. The FBI was informing Brianna's family of the news now. Elle had wanted to go with them, but they refused—not as much out of policy as concern for her safety.

"You ready for more bad news?"

"Can it get worse?"

"You should sit down."

Her father flipped on the TV. Bentley's face flashed across the screen. He was doing a formal interview with one of the local news stations.

Bentley's face glistened with sweat, and Elle clearly recognized the look in his eyes. Eagerness for revenge.

"The entire campaign is in disarray. People are snapping at each other, afraid to leave the house and even pointing fingers," Bentley told the reporter.

The reporter tilted her head. "You think the campaign is falling apart amid these threats and accusations?"

"I'd definitely say that. How can Senator Philips even concentrate on doing his job as a senator when his house is constantly filled by federal agents? When women continue making allegations of inappropriate relationships?"

"Do you think the senator was involved in the murder of his neighbor in northern Virginia?"

"There are a lot of things he might be guilty of, but murder is not one of them."

At least he had enough scruples to say that.

The blonde reporter leaned toward him, her eyebrows drawn

together in serious curiosity. "Who seems to be the target of these threats?"

"Senator Philips's daughter, Elle. Almost all of the deeds done recently have somehow involved her."

Her father clicked off the TV. "It gets better. This is all making national news now."

"So much for keeping things under wraps." She shook her head. "How could Bentley do this?"

"Revenge. He's conniving. I should have fired him years ago." Her father took a step away. "I'm going to call my lawyer, see what can be done. Bentley is not going to get away with any more mud slinging."

More people being hurt around her. When would it end? Probably not until the killers had Elle in their clutches. Wasn't she the real target here?

She knew how to put an end to all of this.

Elle marched into the living room, which was filled with federal agents. They paused when she stormed into the room. When all of their eyes were on her, she put a hand to her hip, drew in a deep breath and said in an amazingly calm voice, "Why don't you use me to draw these men out?"

Denton popped up from the crowd and stepped toward her. "Bad idea. Worst idea I've heard in a long time, for that matter."

Agent Duffield reached Denton's side. "I have to agree. You're not a trained officer of the law. I don't even want to think about how that could turn out."

"Do we have any other choice? These men are just going to keep on killing! They're just going to keep on ruining people's lives. We've got to stop them!"

Denton's hand rested on her arm. "We'll figure out who they are. They'll mess up and we'll catch them. Getting yourself killed in the process won't do anyone any good."

"I can't keep on living like this. Something's got to change. This has to end."

Agent Duffield nodded tightly. "I assure you, we're working on this 24/7. This will end. We've got some good leads, many of them thanks to you. You are doing something. You're helping us put these pieces together. Frankly, if this IT guy wasn't so devious, we'd look into hiring him ourselves. Whoever this man is, he's brilliant with a computer. He's changed his identity, hacked into federal computers and seems to manipulate anything having to do with cyber-information as easily as most people can steer a car."

Denton cupped her elbow and led her from the room. They stopped in the hallway, out of earshot of anyone around. "You need to put that idea out of your mind. If you try to lure them out you'll basically just be offering yourself as a sacrifice. There's no guarantee they'll stop killing."

"But…"

"Listen, the FBI has flown their best men in for this. Everyone's taking it seriously. We've got some deranged serial killers out there, terrorizing not only your family but this whole area. Media got word of what's going on and terror is spreading like wildfire. Everyone thinks this is top priority. Do you understand?"

"I understand, but—"

He stepped closer and held up a finger to her lips. "No 'buts,' Elle. You've already done a tremendous amount to help, just like Agent Duffield said. Don't be headstrong or foolhardy."

Foolhardy. She couldn't deny the claim. Her emotions had her feeling impulsive.

"This, too, will pass. It may not feel like it, but it will."

Elle nodded, a new sense of somberness weighing her down. "I'm going to let you work."

He squeezed her arm. "You okay?"

"No, but I will be." Even she wasn't exactly sure what her words meant. But she knew the truth in them. Everything would work out. But just how many more lives would be lost before then?

Elle was crafting a terse press release—one that she would never send out, but that served to release some of her emotions—when Denton walked into the room with a tall blond man she'd never seen before. Elle paused at her desk, wondering what was going on. She slipped off her reading glasses and stood, straightening her rumpled black pants and button-up shirt.

Denton stepped forward. "Elle, I've got to go somewhere for a few hours, so I'm leaving my associate, Brandon Smith, here until I get back."

Tension squeezed her chest, and she lowered herself back into her chair. "Where are you going?"

Denton's warm gaze fell on her, but he didn't lose his professional astuteness. "I have something I need to do. You can't come with me, and I refuse to leave you alone."

"But—" She started to stand when Denton gently nudged her back into her seat.

"Elle, the FBI is following a lead right now. I'm hoping all of this will be over soon. Until then, you've got to stay put. Promise me you'll stay here."

Almost over? Could that possibly be true? She slumped in the chair. "Of course I'll stay here. I've got lots of damage control to do, anyway."

"Smith will take good care of you until I get back."

Elle glanced at the man from the corner of her eye. Tall, built like a soldier with a buzz cut popular among military men. Finally, she nodded. "Be safe."

Denton's gaze remained on her a moment too long. "I will. We'll talk when I get back."

After Denton left, Elle pointed toward a couch against the wall and said to Smith, "Feel free to have a seat. I'm just going to be right here working on some computer stuff for a while."

"I'll stand." He took a place against the wall, reminding Elle a bit of the guards outside Buckingham Place in London.

She tried to focus on the press release, tried to find a way to spin Bentley's words so that her father's campaign wouldn't blow up. The truth was she didn't care about the campaign anymore. Her friend was dead. Other innocent people had died.

And she'd never really cared about politics anyway.

She leaned back in her seat for a moment. What would her life be like if she quit politics once this election was over? If she did something that truly ignited the passion inside her? What if she actually started that nonprofit she'd thought about?

Elle would be able to help people during the agonizing time while a loved one was missing. She had the whole foundation planned out in her mind. She'd have counselors on hand if they wanted to talk, cooks to provide meals, and herself and others like her to offer wisdom as people who'd been in their shoes before. They could have a hotline number so if they ever needed to talk, someone would be there for them.

Elle wished she had something like that now as she mourned the death of her dear friend. It still didn't seem real that Brianna could be gone. She half expected when she woke up to find this was a nightmare.

Her heart panged with grief. What would she do without her friend? Without someone to share her secrets and her fears? And how could life ever resume to normal without Brianna there to make things more interesting?

Emily. Elle had felt the same way after Emily had died. She knew that life took on a new normal, a normal without your loved one there.

How people could take the lives of innocent people still perplexed and angered her.

And where did Denton have to rush off to? Was he with the FBI following their lead? She doubted it. He'd said earlier that his job was to keep an eye on her. So what was so important that he was leaving all of a sudden?

She glanced back at her temporary bodyguard before standing and stretching. She'd go check on her mom and dad—do something to keep her mind off the matters at hand. She breezed out of the room, noticing that Agent Smith shadowed her, as he was supposed to do.

She missed Denton. She'd gotten used to his presence and his companionship. Soon—she hoped—these killers would be behind bars, and Denton would be out of her life. Why did her heart sink at the thought? Denton was her bodyguard, nothing more. She shouldn't feel attached to him.

He was a risk-taker.

She felt the need to constantly remind herself of that fact. Even if circumstances were different—if he wasn't someone simply hired to be around her—a relationship between them would be impossible. He wasn't her type.

She'd say he wasn't the marrying type, but he'd proved her wrong there.

Could a man who lived for adventure actually be content being with one woman for the rest of his life? She wasn't sure. A month ago she would have said no.

She detoured by her father's office to grab some papers she'd left in there. A piece of trash on the floor caught her eyes. She picked it up, ready to toss it in the garbage when her eyes grazed the words. A receipt from a restaurant in D.C. Two dinners.

She started to crumble it when the date caught her eye. She blinked, unsure if she'd read it correctly. Sure enough, the receipt was dated for a time when her father had assured her he wasn't up in D.C.—around the time when Nancy Green had been killed.

Could her father have something to do with all of this? No. She shook her head. The thought was crazy.

But why would he lie?

She stuck the paper into her pocket and walked toward the kitchen, each step feeling like a lead weight was attached to her feet.

She stopped cold in the entryway to the kitchen. In the distance—through the kitchen and into the sunroom—she spotted her mom and dad sitting together on the couch, talking and laughing. She couldn't remember the last time she'd seen the two of them look so normal and relaxed together. Usually they were both going in different directions, acting like roommates more than husband and wife.

She approached them and lowered herself into a seat across from them. Their faces were practically beaming as their laughter died and they looked her way.

"Hello, darling." Her mom's expression turned somber and compassionate. "How are you holding up today?"

Elle shrugged. "I'm hanging in." Her gaze fell on the space between her parents, and she saw their fingers intertwined.

"There's something I—we—need to tell you, Elle." Her father leaned forward. Lines formed on his forehead and wrinkles branched out from the corners of his eyes. "Elle, I'm considering dropping out of the race for reelection."

She blinked several times, not sure if she'd heard him correctly. "Really? You love politics. This is what you've wanted for—for your whole life, it seems."

His lips pulled into a tight line. "Nothing definite. But I'm seriously considering it. The toll all this has put on the family feels unbearable." He glanced at her mom. "And your mom and I can't stop thinking about—what if that had been you out in the woods instead of Brianna?" He shook his head, his eyelids heavy. "I couldn't bear the thought of losing another daughter, Elle.

"Politics has nearly torn this family apart, Elle. It was bad before these madmen came into our lives. But now all the negatives have tripled—if not more. What would it be like to just try to live a normal life for a while?"

Elle's heart perked. Really? A normal life sounded great. Perfect. Welcome. But so unlike her father. Was there more to his story? The receipt seemed to burn in her pocket. "Could I talk to you for a second, Dad?"

"Of course."

She swallowed. "Alone."

Her father stood and they walked toward the foyer.

"Dad, what's this about?" She pulled out the evidence that he'd been in D.C. "I want to hear it from you. The truth."

Her father's controlled expression disappeared for a moment. Elle had caught him, she realized. Her heart dropped at the thought. All of these years, all of the rumors…she'd tried to deny her father's unfaithfulness. But now she couldn't ignore the facts before her.

"Elle." He looked down at his hands and shook his head, the picture of regret. "You're right. I did go up to D.C. I'm sorry that I lied to you."

"You went to meet Nancy?" The words burned her throat as she said them.

He pulled up his gaze. "No, Elle, I didn't go to meet Nancy."

"Then why?"

"Someone has been trying to convince me to teach a class at George Washington University. We met to discuss the details. I didn't want to mention it because I didn't know what I should do."

"Giving up politics is a big deal. Especially at this stage in the game. The election is only a couple weeks away. There's no time to plug someone else in."

He heaved in a deep breath. "I know. But sometimes what needs to be done simply needs to be done."

"Think about it, Dad. I'll support you either way."

Her dad nodded, his expression still serious and his gaze heavy. "I know. Thank you, darling."

Elle stepped away, one mystery solved but the biggest and most dangerous one still looming.

Denton gave his commissioned piece one last glance before snapping the box closed and placing it in his pocket. "Thanks, Will. This is perfect."

The old man behind the counter smiled, raising the small optical magnifying glass attached to a band at his head. "Glad you like it."

He patted his jacket, his eyes grazing the miscellaneous equipment and inventions Will had laying on tables, hanging on the walls, cluttering the floor. Despite the disorganization, Will was one of the most brilliant men he knew. They'd met when Denton was working for the CIA, and Denton had remained in contact with him since then. "Have I told you that you're amazing?"

"You can't tell me that enough. I'm considering making compliments a part of my fee." He leaned across the counter, his loose, wrinkled skin distorting the tattoos he had emblazing every inch of his arms. "I guess I can't ask what's going on."

"You could, but—"

"You'd have to kill me. Never gets old, saying that, does it?" He straightened and chuckled, grabbing a rag and wiping the glass surface of the counter.

Denton grinned. "Never." He extended his hand. "It's always a pleasure."

"You've got a smile on your face that I haven't seen in a while. Since Wendi, actually. Anything you want to tell me?"

Denton paused, his heart pounding erratically. "Just doing a job."

Will raised a shaggy eyebrow. "Looks like more than a job to me."

"Don't get personally involved. I think you taught me that rule."

"The heart sometimes dictates differently, now, doesn't it?"

"I guess it does." Denton nodded, pondering the wisdom in his words. Even if his words were true, there was a difference between what you felt and how you acted.

Will winked and clucked his tongue. "Keep that spring in your step. I like it. You deserve it after everything you've been through."

"I'll keep that in mind."

Did he really have a new spring in his step? Was he ready for a relationship? Would another woman in his life betray Wendi's memory?

No, Wendi loved him. She would want him to be happy and not to spend the rest of his life alone. She'd even whispered that message to him shortly before breathing her last breath.

His heart clenched at the thought of that dreadful day. Even though Wendi knew Jesus and was going to a better place, the moment was still so heartbreaking. All the hopes they'd had for a life together had disappeared. Denton wasn't sure how he would pick up the pieces of the life he'd built, which then lay in crumbles around him.

Thankfully he'd had good friends in his life—friends like Jack and Will.

He'd kept women at arm's length since then. In all honesty, he hadn't met a woman that he wanted to let closer.

Until Elle.

Elle had captured his thoughts. All he wanted was to be

close to her—not just because of his job, but because she fascinated him. Her smile could light up a room. Though she could easily act spoiled or privileged or even arrogant, she was none of those things. She remained down-to-earth and approachable.

He climbed into his SUV, still oddly aware of the box in his jacket. How would Elle react to it? He wasn't sure. He just knew this was the only thing he could think of to ensure her safety. When he saw the fire in her eyes, he realized she was exactly the type of person who might take matters into her own hands.

And, if she did, he'd be right there. Tracking her.

His cell phone beeped, and he put the device to his ear. Agent Duffield. Had they found the killers? He prayed that was the case.

"Bad news."

Denton braced himself.

"The whole place was wired. As soon as my agents opened the door, the building went up in flames."

Denton squeezed his eyes shut. No more pain or death. There'd been too much of that already. This had to end. "Was anyone hurt?"

"A couple went to the hospital with minor injuries. We approached with caution, fearing something like this. It's like these guys have been two steps ahead of us for every part of the investigation."

This supported Denton's theory that the person behind this was probably working closely somehow with the police or the family.

"I'm on my way back now. Thanks for letting me know."

"In all my years with the FBI, I don't remember two guys this aggressive. I don't know what it's going to take to stop them."

"Something will stop them. We'll get them. Some way, somehow, we'll get them."

With each second, that possibility seemed further away, though.

But he had to hold on to the hope that the end was in sight. He prayed it was.

SIXTEEN

Elle wasn't sure why she felt so anxious for a moment alone with Denton. She knew he was safe, that the explosion hadn't injured him.

Since he'd been back at the house, he'd briefly told her hello and checked to make sure she was okay. Then he'd disappeared into the fray of agents in her living room. She could tell the urgency of the situation had been kicked up a notch higher. These guys were playing with everyone, trying to prove they were smarter than the authorities.

If there was one thing the authorities didn't like, it was someone who thought they were smarter.

Had the FBI finally met their match?

The sun began to sink lower and a few of the agents slipped away, leaving only a handful. Eventually, the house quieted. Elle changed into some yoga pants and a long-sleeved T-shirt. She escaped into the library to read a book and decompress. She started a little blaze in the gas fireplace and dimmed the lights. The temperature had dropped along with the sun, and an autumn chill seemed to creep into the house.

Reading by firelight seemed relaxing enough. But in the quiet, her thoughts turned to Brianna, and tears began escaping down her cheeks. She wiped at them and leaned into the couch with her face toward the flames. She missed Denton.

As much as she didn't want to admit it, she did. She'd gotten used to their nightly chats here in the library, and she would have been lying not to admit to herself that she hoped to see him tonight, also.

Her heart sped when she heard a knock. She looked up from her book and saw Denton standing there, his trademark rakish grin spread across his face. Elle pulled herself up and lowered her book as Denton took a seat beside her on the couch.

"Taking a break?"

He shrugged. "A short one. These guys are really getting under the FBI's skin."

"Mine, too." She leaned back and exhaled slowly. "Sometimes I don't feel like this is ever going to end."

"It will." He shifted and his gaze locked on hers. He wiped away some leftover moisture on her cheeks, the action causing her to catch her breath. "Did I catch you at a bad time?"

She shook her head. "No, some company actually sounds good right now."

"Thinking about Brianna?"

She nodded. "It doesn't seem real yet."

He leaned forward. "Elle, I have something I want to give you."

Elle twisted her lips in confusion and apprehension. "Okay."

"Listen, I know how much that necklace your grandmother gave you meant to you. And I know the message behind the necklace made it even more special. The dove represented hope, and hope is something we all need. You especially need it right now with everything that's going on."

Her hand went to her throat again, as it often did when she thought about the heirloom. Her neck felt bare without the jewelry. "Aside from taking away the people in my life, that was probably the next worst thing someone could take from me. I don't know if I'll ever get it back, which just makes me heartsick."

He reached into his coat pocket and pulled out a jewelry box. "That's why I wanted to give you this." He opened the box and a replica of the necklace rested there against the black fabric.

She gasped, simultaneous to tears popping to her eyes. "Wow…that's just beautiful." She reached for it and let her finger trace the dove's outline. "How…?"

He shrugged. "I have connections."

"Denton, I don't know what to say. This is one of the nicest things someone could have done for me. Thank you."

He took the box and pulled out the necklace. He held the ends toward her. "May I?"

She swooped up her hair. "Yes, please do."

He leaned forward and Elle was oddly aware of his closeness, of his familiar cologne. Her skin tingled as his fingers brushed her neck.

Finally, he clasped the necklace together and leaned back, a soft grin on his face. "Looks good."

She touched the precious metal at her neck. "Thank you."

"It's the least I could do."

"Why? You don't owe me anything. You didn't have to do this." Her heart beat in her ears as she waited for his response.

"I wanted to."

"Why?"

His finger brushed her cheek. "Because…"

Her heart stammered in her chest at his nearness. She wanted to reach out and touch him, also, to wrap her arms around his neck and pull him closer. She wanted to feel the scruff on his face and absorb his tantalizing cologne. "Yes?"

"Because I love seeing you smile." His voice sounded husky and warm. He stroked her cheek again. "And hearing you laugh. And seeing your eyes light up with hope."

"You're sweet."

His gaze looked smoldering. "Elle...?"

"Yes?" Every cell of her body seemed aware of Denton.

Before she said anything else, his lips covered hers. Tingles traveled down her spine and then back up again. Her hands curled around his neck.

Kissing Denton felt natural. It felt right. And it felt like something she'd wanted to do for a long time.

They pulled away and stared at each other a moment.

Finally, Elle cleared her throat. "The unromantic, pragmatic side of me feels the need to ask what that was."

"Do I really need to explain?" His eyes sparkled.

"You know how I feel about relationships." How they terrified her, how she'd rather work in politics the rest of her life than date the wrong man again.

"You're cautious. Rightfully so." He stroked her cheek with his fingertips, the motion gentle and sweet and causing shudders again.

But she had to get back to the matter at hand. "So what was that? A spontaneous mistake? An impulsive moment we should forget?"

Denton kneaded the tight muscles at the base of her neck. "How about the invitation to explore a relationship?"

"I just don't like guessing." Or taking risks.

"I can respect that. Sometimes you've just got to trust your heart. What's your heart tell you?"

That you're perfect, someone I could spend the rest of my life with, and a man I'd be content to grow old and gray with together.

Lingering beneath the giddiness she felt was fear. Could she really trust her heart? She wasn't sure.

"Wherever you set foot, you will be on land I have given you.... No one will be able to stand against you as long as

you live. For I will be with you as I was with Moses. I will not fail you or abandon you."

The Bible verse repeated in her mind as Denton pulled her into his arms and they settled back on the couch.

"I'm not good at relationships, Denton." The words croaked out. "They scare me almost as much as the men trying to claim my life."

"How about we take it slow? If you start freaking out, then you talk to me about it. Can you handle that?"

I will not fail you or abandon you. No matter where she went or what she did, she had to trust in God's presence in her life. She nodded. "I think I can handle that."

But even as she said the words, she knew they were easier said than done.

Denton slipped an arm around the back of the pew and rubbed Elle's shoulder. He could tell by the way her chin trembled that she was trying to hold it together. Elle was good at that—trying to hold everything together even if she was falling apart. She'd always been there for other people, even if it meant giving up her own desires. More than anything, Denton wanted her to have the chance to pursue her own dreams and passions.

The pastor concluded his eulogy, wrapping up Jimmy's life. His life wasn't one that got much attention, but it was well-lived. He left behind a grieving family who'd obviously loved him, and a string of selfless acts that several people had stood at the pulpit and talked about.

That's what Denton wanted one day. No matter how impossible the dream might feel at times, he wanted a family to go home to. He wanted to feel chubby toddler arms around his neck one day and have a wife to lie beside in bed at night.

He'd thought his dreams had come true with Wendi. But Wendi had just been one, wonderful part of his life. He still had open miles of future before him. He'd like Elle to be a part of that future.

The thought of her sweet smile, the tenderness in her gaze, the way she thought of others before herself, all tugged at his heart. But he also knew that there was fear simmering beneath the surface, fear over relationships and being hurt and picking the wrong guy again. He also knew her selflessness could get her in trouble. He wanted to do everything within his power to keep her safe—to shelter and protect her for a long time.

A tear drizzled down her cheek. He pulled a tissue from the box beside him and handed it to her. She dabbed her eyes. He didn't have to ask to know her thoughts. First Jimmy's funeral. Before long, Brianna's funeral. She'd already been through both her sister's and her grandmother's.

Wendi's funeral came to mind. It had been one of the hardest days of his life. Thankfully he'd had good friends at his side, supporting him and encouraging him. He hadn't wanted to let Wendi go. He remembered her coffin being lowered into the ground. The memory still caused an ache in his heart.

It was a reminder that we weren't promised tomorrow, so we had to make the most of today.

As the funeral wrapped up, he once again dragged his gaze around the room, looking for signs of anyone suspicious. He had other agents stationed around the perimeter of the sanctuary, and the FBI had a presence, also. Just in case.

Elle looked up at him and offered a fleeting smile, her eyes still red-rimmed. "He was a good man," she mumbled. "He didn't deserve to go like this."

"No one does." He wanted nothing more than to sweep her into his arms and soothe away her sorrows. But he couldn't. Not here. Not now. Instead, he settled on rubbing her neck muscles. "You ready to go?"

She nodded. They'd already decided to skip the graveside service. They'd shown their respect and now it was time to let the family have some time to mourn, away from body-guards and federal agents.

Denton led her to his SUV outside and cranked the engine. "You ready to go back to the house?"

"I'm losing my mind being there all the time."

His hand covered her knee. "What's going on, Elle? Talk to me."

"Those men may not have harmed me physically yet, but they're tormenting me emotionally. I'm letting them keep me locked away. They're winning, Denton."

"If you leave and live your regular life, you're going to let them win because they'll have you in their crosshairs."

"I just keep having terrible nightmares, and I wake up and feel like I'm suffocating. They're playing this psychological game with me, and I feel defeated. Everyone keeps on saying they'll be caught soon. Well, they still haven't been caught. Sometimes, I don't think they'll ever be caught, and that people are just going to keep on dropping like flies around me."

Denton kept his hand on her knee and waited for her to continue, to get her emotions out. She closed her eyes, still wet with tears, and lowered her head. She used a rumpled tissue in her hands to dab her eyes again. Her strained gaze looked forward. "Sorry about that."

"Don't apologize for being real."

She blinked and turned toward him. "What did you say?"

"To not apologize for being real. I want you to be yourself around me."

She sucked in a breath before letting out a slow, half-hearted chuckle. "There's only been one person in my life who's ever encouraged me to be myself. My grandmother. Everyone else has always pushed me to be the person they want me to be. The cultured beauty queen, the poised politician's daughter, the astute student. I've never felt like people want me to be who I am." She reached forward and rested her hand on his cheek. Just feeling her touch caused lava to flow through him.

"Thank you, Denton."

He shoved down the urge to pull her into his arms and drink in her scent. "I mean it, Elle. Don't ever feel like you have to be someone you're not when you're around me." He ran his thumb gently under her eye, wiping away the moisture there. "There is somewhere we can go to get you out of the house for a while."

"Where?"

"Do you trust me?"

Denton sensed her hesitation, sensed the way she had to process his question. "Yes, I trust you," she finally said. Would she ever fully trust him with her heart, though?

"Let me make a phone call, and then we'll go. Deal?"

"Deal."

Elle had it bad. Denton was the kind of man she'd been dreaming about…well, forever. She could seriously get used to having him in her life, to looking into those warm brown eyes, to smelling his aftershave. She had to remember to use her head, to keep her eyes open for signs that Denton was like the rest of the men in her life.

No, he was different. Or was he?

She couldn't be certain. Not yet. Could she ever be certain?

Thirty minutes later, they drove down the road to a nearby beach called Sandbridge. Mostly locals knew of this beach, unlike the resort area, which was crowded with vacationers and high-rise hotels. "The beach?"

"You mentioned once how much you enjoyed it."

Elle's heart leaped in a way it shouldn't—not if it wanted to stay safe. "That I did."

They followed the shoreline until they came to a stop at a large house located on the beachfront. "Yours?"

"No way. I don't get paid that well. It belongs to a guy I work with named Bradley Stone. He said we could use it." He opened his door. "Wait there. I'll come and get you."

She didn't have a chance to argue as he hurried around the vehicle to her door. He helped her out, his gaze surveying the area. Apprehension immediately gripped her as she exited the vehicle. Had the madmen followed them? Was she putting others in danger?

Denton's hand went to her back and he led her up the external stairs to the second level of the home. He pulled out a key and quickly ushered her inside the lush beachfront home. Elle's gaze scanned the place. "He must make some serious money at Eyes."

"He works developing new products that he sells to the military. He's brilliant and tough." Denton shrugged off his jacket, pulled away his tie and rolled up his sleeves.

Elle had to look away before he caught her approving stare. "Sounds like it."

"This place is a favorite for company parties." In two steps, he was at her side. Heat rushed through her. Why did the man have this effect on her? He seemed to sense Elle's reaction and grinned. "Want to go outside for a minute?"

"Sounds perfect."

They sat on the deck overlooking the ocean for a moment, staring at the massive beauty around them. The day hovered around fifty-five degrees, not too cold, but not warm enough to go without a coat. Plus, the air was bound to be cooler with the breeze coming off the ocean. The salty air surrounded them as seagulls whined, looking for food. Elle spotted at least five of Denton's men, each dressed casually for the occasion. But beneath their sunglasses, she knew they were watching carefully for something out of the ordinary.

Agent Smith climbed the steps with a box in hand. "Delivery for one Mark Denton."

"Thanks, Smith." Denton took the box from him, and familiar aromas began to tantalize Elle. When Denton opened the box, she saw her favorite pizza—basil, artichoke, pesto, mushrooms and fresh mozzarella.

"You remembered?"

He smiled. "Of course. Dig in."

"This was so incredibly sweet. Thank you." Despite the craziness around them, Elle, just for a moment, enjoyed herself eating her favorite pizza in one of her favorite places. Her thoughts didn't stay carefree for long, though. There was too much at stake to let down her guard and fully enjoy herself. "Brianna always hated this pizza, you know. When it came to pizza, she was totally traditional. I think that was one of the only areas of her life where she valued tradition, however."

"The two of you were opposites?"

"Yeah, I guess you could say that." It was hard to believe that they'd never have another argument over what to get on their pizza again. How could that chapter of her life have closed so swiftly and without warning? "My dad's thinking about dropping out of the race." Elle hadn't intended on bringing it up, but the fact had popped out. Maybe thinking about her father's career was better than dwelling on Brianna at the moment.

Denton pulled up his head in surprise. "Really?"

"I can't believe it. I think he's finally realizing that success can come at a price."

"And he's realizing that family is invaluable?"

"That's how it seems." She sucked in a deep breath, her thoughts as scattered as the seagulls up and down the shoreline. There was so much to process, to try to comprehend. Somehow being here at the beach with Denton and her favorite pizza soothed her spirit—temporarily, at least. "The ocean always helps to relax me somehow. When my problems seem big, I always look out at the water and think that the God who created that vast beauty is much bigger than anything this world deals me."

"The world's been dealing you a lot lately."

They sat in silence for a few minutes until dark clouds rolled in the distance and the breeze turned chilly. She rubbed her arms. "You mind if we head inside?"

He grabbed the pizza box and ushered her through the patio doors. Elle stood at the window, watching the ocean, when Denton wrapped his arms around her from behind. She wanted to melt in his embrace, but she held back.

"What are you afraid of, Elle?" He asked the question so softly that she almost thought she imagined it.

Her throat constricted. "What do you mean?"

He turned her around until she faced him. His face was only inches from hers, and each perfectly chiseled feature seemed to beckon her fingers to graze them. She wanted to wrap her arms around his neck, to forget her fears, her heartbreak. But she couldn't.

His warm eyes implored hers. "Why is it that every time we get close, you look like a scared rabbit ready to run?"

She wanted to take a step back but couldn't. Denton's arms were wrapped firmly around her waist. She had no choice but to answer the question. She cleared her throat before meeting her gaze. "Relationships scare me. Forever scares me. Failing scares me. Of all the things I could fail at, marriage isn't one I want to risk. I'm not as naive as I used to be."

Denton kept one arm at her waist but released the other hand to stroke her cheek. "He really broke your heart, didn't he?"

Her knees felt weak at his touch. "Broke my heart? Why do you think that?" Even as she said the words, she knew the answer. She was just buying herself time to conjure up a response and to keep her composure.

He shrugged. "A hunch."

"Preston liked to take risks, so I should have realized that would carry over into his relationships, too."

"Not every man is like him, you know." Denton's eyes caught hers. Those brown, beautiful eyes that always seemed to draw her in.

She had to get a grip, to get back to reality. She tried to take a step back but, again, Denton held her, unwilling to let her brush off this conversation. "He was kind of like you. You live for risks, don't you? It's what makes you good at your job."

He leaned toward her. "I'm nothing like your ex-fiancé, Elle. When I see something good, I hold on to it."

Her cheeks flushed and, for a moment, she was speechless. She believed him. She really did. And that realization terrified her. "I know, Denton. My head knows, at least. My heart has a hard time keeping up."

"Your odds for staying married are better than a lot of the other odds you've faced. Getting into Yale…what are those odds? One in five hundred? Winning the title Miss Virginia?"

"I grasp the odds. I realize the flaw in my thinking. It's not my thinking that holds me back. It's my heart that can't be convinced."

"With time it will be." His words sounded so confident. His eyes went to her lips. He traced their outline with his finger.

She thought her emotions for Preston had been strong, but they were nothing compared to how she felt with Denton. Was it possible to feel swept away and grounded in the same moment? To feel blissfully respected and cared for and protected?

She wasn't sure who stepped closer or who initiated the kiss. She only knew that when Denton's lips covered hers, time seemed to stop. When he drew her closer and the kiss deepened, her head spun and her heart danced.

Could this really be the man she'd been waiting for, the man who would prove her fears unfounded?

Was she brave enough to find out?

She didn't know.

SEVENTEEN

Elle and Denton arrived back at the house in time to see FBI agents clearing their command post. All of the investigations would be done from their office from here on out. They had a lead on the IT guy that they were investigating.

While Denton disappeared into the library to handle a situation that had arisen at Eyes's headquarters, Elle slipped into her office and spent the rest of the day researching nonprofits, writing mission statements and dreaming. She'd promised her grandmother that she wouldn't let her fears hold her back. Was she willing to task a risk this big and start this nonprofit?

If there was one thing she'd learned from the threats on her life, it was that life was short. It could end twenty years from now, or it could end tomorrow. No one, except God, knew the day or the hour. She'd had a moment of clarity at the bank as the gun was held to her head. Life was short. You had to make the most of every moment. By following everyone else's plan for her life, she wasn't living to the fullest extent. She had to make some changes.

Starting with her career in politics.

It wasn't that she wished for her father to end his campaign run and his senate career—that was his decision and she'd support him either way. It was simply that she didn't want to be a part of it anymore. She'd become jaded and burned-out. She wanted to pursue the things she loved. Life was too short not to.

Somehow, being with Denton seemed to ignite something in her. It stirred up her fire for following her dreams.

She smiled as she thought about their kiss earlier. It was perfect and sweet. Tender yet passionate. Denton was the kind of man who could easily sweep her off her feet.

And that thought simultaneously thrilled and terrified her.

Her phone beeped. She'd gotten a new phone after the FBI confiscated her old one. She should have given out the new number to members of the press, but instead she'd given them her office line. She didn't feel like constantly being on call. She had other things to worry about…like staying alive. She turned on the screen and saw she had a new text message. She scrunched her eyebrows together at the unknown number.

She clicked on the message and some pictures came on the screen. Too small to make out, she used her touch screen to enlarge the first one.

She sucked in a breath.

Denton.

With another woman.

Laughing together at Fred's Seafood, the same place where he'd taken her.

His forehead was bandaged, so these pictures had to be taken after the guardhouse explosion. Elle's heart twisted in pain and regret. "No…" she whispered.

She didn't want to see the next picture, but she couldn't stop herself. The image showed Denton walking outside of Fred's with the same woman, hand in hand. The next picture showed them kissing against a car. The woman was super-model beautiful—long and lean with tresses of blond hair flowing down her back. Both glowed with obvious affection for each other.

Tears rushed to her eyes. When Denton had slipped out

yesterday and left her in someone else's care, this is what he'd been doing? Then why in the world did he come back and kiss her? Was it just for the thrill of the hunt?

She shook her head. Nothing made sense. Or did everything make sense? Had she fallen for the wrong man again? Were old habits hard to break?

The most obvious answer was usually the correct one.

And, in this case, it meant that, yes, she'd been taken for a fool…again.

Denton slipped his cell phone back into his pocket, glad to have some confusion at Eyes's headquarters resolved. He wandered down the hallway, looking for Elle. He found her in her office, staring at her phone with a blank expression. She didn't even look up when he walked in.

"Did you get another message?"

She continued looking straight ahead. "You could say that." Her voice lacked emotion, and that scared Denton. What was going on?

He pulled up a chair next to her and sat down. "What's going on? What's wrong?"

"You had me fooled." Fire danced in her eyes.

"What are you talking about?"

She held up her cell phone. Denton's eyes widened as he absorbed the images. Each shot felt like a blow to the heart. "Where did you get those?"

"An innocent man would have denied the picture's authenticity right away. I guess that answers my question."

He could hardly focus on what she said. "Where did someone get those pictures?"

"You tell me. It looks like at Fred's Seafood. Based on your injury, it was taken yesterday when you stepped out. Why'd you lead me on, Denton? I thought you were different." Her voice cracked, the weight of her pain seeping into his heart. He had to ignore his own aching heart right now and think about Elle.

His gaze transformed from somber to compassionate. "Elle, I can explain...."

She stood and shook her head. "Save it. I've heard all the explanations before. Too many times, for that matter."

Denton grabbed her hand and pulled her back down into her chair. "No, really, Elle. These are pictures of me and... me and my wife."

Elle froze. Blinked. Shook her head. "You can't even imagine the thoughts going through my mind right now."

"Elle, that's Wendi. It was taken six years ago."

Elle said nothing as, most likely, she contemplated whether his words were the truth or the excuse of a man caught cheating. Her voice was even, steady, when she finally said, "The cut on your forehead. It's the one you got a few days ago from the explosion. It's in that picture, practically date-stamping it."

He pointed to the phone, at Wendi's picture. "Elle, you've got to believe me. Someone tampered with this image. Look at it. You can tell in the picture that I'm younger. My hair's a little different, even."

Elle swallowed, her fingers going to the necklace as they always did. "You're saying that this computer genius tampered with photos he pulled off your computer? That it wasn't enough to attempt to kill me, but now he's got to mess with my heart, also?" Her already fragile, untrusting heart that was just looking for an excuse to stop trusting Denton, too.

He tried to pull her into a hug, but she shook her head and stepped back. "You've got to have trust to have a relationship, Denton. I obviously don't have that yet. I've been burned too many times."

"Elle—"

"I just...I just need some time alone." She nodded toward her cell. "You can see if the FBI can have the text traced. I'm sure they won't be able to, but it can't hurt to try. I...I need to lie down."

"Elle." His hand reached for her shoulder.

She brushed it off. "I'm sorry. I just...I just don't know anything right now."

Upstairs, Elle laid down on her bed, exhaustion weighing on her. Not only did her burdens feel physical and emotional, but now her heart had gotten involved on a romantic level—on what she'd thought to be a romantic level, at least. In the end, it was all heartbreak.

She'd known that would be the outcome. Wasn't it always? Denton had fit the personality profile perfectly. She'd foolishly thought he was different. But he wasn't—was he? Or was this really about her trust issues with men? Would she ever get over these issues or would her fears ruin every future relationship?

Something crinkled underneath her pillow. She sat up and reached for whatever it was. Her hand emerged with an envelope.

Instantly, her guard went up. Carefully, she pulled open the seal and slipped out a folded piece of paper. Inside, a typewritten message waited.

There's a way to end this madness, Ellebird. You can trade your own life for the lives of those around you. Go to this website and enter: ELLEBIRD, FUNERAL. You'll find instructions there. If you decide not to come, remember—their blood is on your hands.

Their blood is on your hands.

A sob rose from deep within her at the thought, at the implications.

Her gaze skittered around the room. How had this note gotten here? How had the killer managed to get into her house undetected? Not just into her house—into her room. Her bed.

Her blood went cold at the thought.

If she offered herself or not, she could be dead. In the blink of an eye. Wasn't that how quickly things could change?

If she didn't this madness could continue…for how long? Was there really an end in sight? The men seemed to be brilliant, brazen and disgustingly evil. Their tirade would continue until they got what they wanted.

And apparently, what they wanted was Elle.

She closed her eyes as images of what would happen once she was in their clutches flashed through her mind. Torture. Agony. No, these men wouldn't offer her a fast death. They'd come too far for that.

She could tell the FBI agents downstairs. Denton. Her father.

She was sure they'd all jump right on it.

But to no avail.

They were dealing with people who'd outsmarted all of them. Who could apparently walk through walls. Who knew their next step before they did. Who had the magic of technology at their fingertips.

She could turn over the information with hopes of finding a lead.

Or she could end this whole nightmare.

No, no, no, no.

She couldn't hand herself over to killers. She shuddered to think what they might do to her.

But could she sit idly by while everyone around her suffered? Innocent people? Who would be next?

She slipped the letter back into the envelope and walked to her dresser. Where was her laptop? She always kept it in her room.

She closed her eyes. Except that she'd taken it downstairs

earlier. She needed to access that website. See what information was there.

How would she get downstairs without Denton taking note? She didn't know.

But before she made any decisions, she'd check the website. She had to.

Because her heart couldn't take putting anyone else in her life in danger.

Elle's hand trembled on the stair railing as she tiptoed downstairs. Act normal. Act naturally. Tiptoeing and trembling were anything but natural.

She paused before reaching the bottom step, sucked in a deep breath and willed herself to relax. She'd casually walk to her office, get her laptop and escape upstairs again. She could do this without anyone getting suspicious.

Except maybe Denton.

He seemed to have a sense about him. Sometimes it had seemed like he knew her better than she knew herself.

She spotted him across the room, looking a bit distracted for the first time since she'd known him. Maybe seeing that picture of him and his wife had done it. Now that Elle thought about it, that would be jarring. The picture made it obvious that the two had loved each other. Their affection showed in their eyes.

Denton looked up as she breezed past. She didn't stop to talk to anyone—just made a beeline for her office, grabbed her laptop and turned to—

She collided with Denton. "What's going on?"

She swallowed, straightened her shirt, resisted her crazy urge to reach for him. "Nothing's going on. I just need my laptop."

"Can we talk? Really talk?" His voice sounded low and

earnest, and it made Elle want to forget everything else going on. But she couldn't.

She tucked her hair behind her ear, willing herself to remain calm and cool. "There's something I've got to do that can't wait. Maybe later?"

His gaze searched hers, the pain in his eyes making her want to pour everything out. Could he read her thoughts? Did he know what had happened? Because something about the man always made her feel like he could see into her soul.

He nodded. "Later."

She forced a smile and hurried past, up the stairs, into her room where she locked the door. She'd done it. She'd gotten by Denton. Her pulse pounded in her ears, and her breathing felt shallow.

Should she really do this?

Yes, she decided. She should.

Her hands shook so badly against the keyboard that she thought with certainty she'd never get the website address typed. Four tries later, a site popped up. Plain. Just a white background. In the middle of the screen was a place to type the username and password. She typed them in just as they directed.

Another white screen appeared, this one with black letters running across it.

She braced herself for what she might discover here.

Good girl, Ellebird. We knew you'd put the safety of others above your own. I'm sorry it's come down to this, but there's no backing out now. If you tell anyone about this note or website, then we've wired bombs in your parents' and boyfriend's bedrooms. We've already planted listening devices around the house, so leak a word of this, and your parents and Denton will be gone with one push of the button. Understand?

Her chest squeezed with pain. No. This couldn't be happening.

She continued reading, though it felt like her world was spinning.

Go to your car this evening at midnight. We've programmed an address into your GPS. It will tell you where to go. We'll be waiting. Don't be late.

She glanced at her watch. Midnight? That was five hours away.

She covered her face with her hands.

What was she going to do?

Her hands slipped from her face. She knew what she had to do. She had no other choice.

EIGHTEEN

Denton couldn't stop the shock from making him feel both numb and outraged.

How had someone gotten those photos of him and Wendi? He couldn't even remember the last time he'd seen them. One of Wendi's friends was a photographer and had snapped the photos while playing with a new camera. Denton had stored the pictures on his computer—which would explain how someone had gotten them. If one of the men was an IT guy, then he could easily have hacked into Denton's home computer. Based on everything Denton had seen so far, the man was probably a computer genius, for that matter.

Whoever these guys were, they knew exactly what was going on in this investigation. They'd known that to get to Elle, they could send her those pictures and make it look as if Denton wasn't a one-woman man. Even more than that, they knew Elle's fear was falling for a man she couldn't trust. How did they know that?

Her ex-fiancé came to mind. Of course Preston would know that. And with his connections within the family's networks, he could have someone on the inside keeping an eye and ear open for what was going on. There were probably others who knew Elle's history, but Denton was too distracted to think of them. He was still caught up in the memory of the way Elle had looked when she handed him the phone.

He wanted the chance to reassure Elle. But he knew she needed space, and he would respect that. She had been through a lot, and she was no doubt still mourning the loss of her best friend. All the trauma in her life was bound to affect her. She'd put on a good front, but now it seemed as if things were getting to her. No one could fault her for that.

Besides, was he ready to love again? He'd convinced himself that he was. But seeing those pictures of Wendi brought back a fresh wave of emotions and memories.

Was his soul ready for the risks involved? He'd been content with knowing he'd found love once in his life. Could you find a great thing more than once?

He knew the answer—a resounding yes.

He nodded, a seriousness falling over him. He'd thought his heart felt weighed down before. Now it felt anchored with no hopes of dislodging from the heaviness holding it back.

Time. Give her time. Why was that so hard?

At least she seemed content, for lack of a better word, to stay put. He could rest assured that she was safe. That afforded him the opportunity to do some more research on her ex-fiancé and everyone else who had a motive. He had to find these guys in order to begin repairing all the damage they'd already done.

Elle slipped a pocketknife into her shoe. Hid a razor in her back pocket. Donned a bright yellow T-shirt with a black hoodie over it. Squeezed a sample-sized perfume under the band of her watch where she could slip it out and use it as a type of eye irritant if necessary.

No, she wasn't tough. But she was smart. She'd fight for her life. She'd fight for the lives of those she cared about.

The clock read 11:30 p.m. The house had quieted and everyone had slipped to bed. The agents had dispersed for the evening.

But then there was Denton. How she could possibly sneak past him baffled her. He seemed to anticipate her every move. Every squeak coming from the house was on his radar in point-five seconds.

If she could get to the door leading to the garage, she could turn off the house alarm for long enough to get outside to her car. But then there was the matter of starting her car, making it down the driveway, past Denton's agent stationed outside and far enough away that no one would be able to follow her once they noticed she was gone.

Sweat covered her brow just thinking about it.

One wrong move and everyone she loved could die.

What other option did she have?

If she told Denton, the killers would hear her and kill them all.

She'd considered sending Denton a message by email or text, but with the computer expertise these guys were showing, certainly they'd pick up on that also.

She picked up a memo pad. She could leave a handwritten note. That was the one thing the killers couldn't intercept. Writing by hand? Who did that anymore?

She would.

Just a short note, she told herself, to her parents and Denton. She'd tell them how much she loved them and that they should get out of the house ASAP and have the bomb squad come out. She'd tell them she did this for them. And she was sorry, but there was no other way.

At eleven forty-five, she opened her door, praying it wouldn't squeak. It didn't. Using every ounce of willpower, she tiptoed down the hallway. When she reached the end, she paused. She heard nothing.

She'd made it this far. Now she had to see if the rest of her plan would work. She just needed a ten- or fifteen-minute lead time, she'd figured.

Silence surrounded her as she crept down the back stairway. At the landing, she scanned the hallway behind her. Nothing.

Relief and fear filled her. She'd half expected Denton to pop out and ask what she was doing.

Quickly, she punched the security code into the keypad by the door. She tried to mask the beeps by using a cloth to cover the speaker. It worked, but not entirely. She had to move fast.

She slipped outside, grabbed some gasoline from the garage, and hunkered down as she walked to the backyard. Her hands shook as she poured the fluid over the grass twenty feet out from the house.

Her gaze skittered around her. No sign of the night guard.

Using a lighter, she ignited the gas. Flames flared into the nighttime sky, growing by the moment.

"I'm sorry," she whispered.

Wasting no more time, she ran toward her car, parked in the driveway. She stayed close to the house, her heart pounding in her ears.

Checking to see the coast was clear, she crouched until she reached her vehicle. She crawled inside and started the ignition. It purred to life.

The GPS popped on. Sure enough, there were directions waiting for her. They'd somehow managed to program her system.

Lord, help us.

She had no time to waste. She pushed on the accelerator—hard. Her car zoomed forward.

She hit the button resting atop her sun visor, and the gate slowly swung open. She turned hard once she reached the street, and she didn't let up. She wouldn't let up.

Not when the lives of everyone else depended on her.

* * *

Denton's gut had been trying to tell him something all night. He hadn't been able to sleep as he tried to piece together the clues his intuition seemed to offer.

He stood in the library, hands on hips. He'd hoped Elle might come down, but he'd known she wouldn't. She had said she wanted to turn in early.

The insomniac deserved to sleep some. He couldn't argue that.

He snuck downstairs and began scouring articles about past cases Senator Philips had participated in as attorney or judge. There was something in here somewhere. He just had to figure out what.

He lingered on one article. The picture underneath caught his eye. The photo was of a middle-aged couple, trailed by two young adult males. It gave him pause enough to read more.

The article was about the trial of a man accused of killing a young woman named Katrina Matthews. She'd walked into the middle of a drug bust gone bad. One of the drug dealers shot her while trying to evade authorities. The police eventually caught the man. The case went to trial but was thrown out because of a technicality. The police had forgotten to read the man his rights. The family decried the lack of justice for Katrina, and rightfully so. The system had failed them and there'd been little anyone could do about it. It was one of the last cases Senator Philips had judged before being elected to the senate.

Denton blew up the picture, focusing on the two teenage boys. One was shorter, heavier, and the other tall and thin. Just like the bank robbers? He focused on their faces. The taller one seemed familiar, but why and from where?

Thomas and Ryan Matthews. Denton did an internet search for their names.

The older one popped up. The man had a criminal record.

He'd been charged with assault in a domestic dispute. He just got out of jail three months ago. When his sister had been murdered, he'd been in the military…and was an explosives expert. He was discharged for bad conduct.

Denton swallowed. He enlarged the man's mug shot. He was heavier now and his hair was shorter with a tight buzz cut.

He sucked in a breath. He knew where he'd seen the man before. He was part of the Philipses' cleaning service.

He stood just as a subtle sound caught his ear. What was that? It almost seemed like a beeping. The noise was so muted, he wondered if he was hearing things.

He pulled his gun anyway. Cautiously, he started toward the south wing of the house. Just as he reached the door leading into the garage, his cell vibrated. He plucked it from his belt. It was the agent he had stationed outside.

Keeping a watchful eye on everything around him, he put the phone to his ear. "What's going on?"

"We've got a situation in the backyard. A fire."

"Did you see anyone suspicious?"

"No…"

Denton bristled, wondering about his stalled reaction. "What? What is it?"

"A car just took off down the driveway, sir."

His back muscles tensed. "A car? What car?"

"I'm not sure. A silver sedan."

Elle. That was Elle's car. What was she doing?

"Do you want me to go after it?"

Denton shook his head. "No. Let her go. I'll find her. I need you it come inside and evacuate everyone in the house, then check out Elle's room. See if there's anything suspicious there. Understand?"

"Understood, sir."

Denton grabbed his keys from his pocket, punched in the

alarm code—which was probably the noise he'd heard earlier—and ran to his SUV.

He pulled up a website on his cell as he hurried. A couple seconds later, a dot appeared on a map. A moving dot. Elle. He knew her exact location thanks to the tracker he'd had put in her necklace.

He had to get to her before the killers did.

Elle's hand trembled on the steering wheel. Sweat trickled from her forehead and down her temples as the dark road stretched before her, only illuminated by the beam of her headlights.

What was she doing? Was there no other way? Really?

These guys were smart. The GPS would lead her to their location. That meant there'd be no record of where she was going. She had no cell phone for authorities to use to pinpoint where she was. Nothing to guide anyone to help her.

She traveled farther into the backwoods of Virginia Beach, the side that tourists rarely saw.

"Turn right in fifteen feet."

The grating male voice on the GPS nearly sent her through the roof.

She slowed as a street appeared ahead. The road was nothing more than a gravel lane leading into the woods. Here, there were no streetlights. Only her headlights guided her down the narrow road. Rocks popped beneath her tires, rumbling, churning along with her gut.

What was going on back at her parents' house? No doubt the fire had been discovered. She'd set it far enough away that they should be able to douse the flames before its hot fingers reached the building's walls. Certainly they'd discovered she'd already left. Had Denton tried to follow her?

Tears pushed their way out. Would they ever understand why she'd done this? Was it truly the right thing?

She sucked in a deep breath. She had to believe it was, to stop second-guessing herself. She was doing this to preserve the lives of those she loved. She hoped, in the process, to save her own life also. Most would call that foolhardy. She didn't know what she'd call it.

The GPS instructed her to turn left. The road was barely visible, just a sliver through the forest. Huge divots sunk on either side of her car, each filled with black water that caught in the headlights.

Lord, give me strength and wisdom.

"You have reached your destination ahead."

Elle slowed. Chills raced down her spine and then back up again. The woods cleared—just slightly—and on the other side stood a house. The building was white, run-down and rickety. This was where she was supposed to go?

Something rang in her car. Was that a phone? Whose?

She reached under the seat, felt beneath the console before finally opening the glove compartment. The screen of a shiny plastic cell phone illuminated the small space. Where...?

Of course. These men had thought of everything. No aspect of her demise had been forgotten.

The phone barely stayed in her hands thanks to her shaky, jerking muscles. With a dry throat and a voice that didn't sound like her own she answered, "Hello?"

"Good girl, Ellebird. You came this far. There's a path behind the house. Follow it. We'll give you more instructions as you go."

She sucked in a deep breath, and stepped from the car.

Here goes nothing.

Only her life didn't feel like nothing. These men were sure to treat her like it was, though.

NINETEEN

Denton flew down the road, praying no cops tried to pull him over for speeding. The FBI wasn't far behind. They were going to catch these guys before anything happened to Elle. They had to. There was no other option as far as Denton was concerned.

The road became narrower, darker and more ominous. Where had they taken her? Just what were they planning?

He swerved onto a gravel road, quickly slowing in order to not miss the directions on his cell phone screen. The end destination appeared to be in the middle of nowhere.

His phone rang. Agent Duffield. Maybe he knew something that Denton didn't. "What's going on?"

"Your room and the senator's bedroom were both wired. The house has been evacuated. We also found a note in Elle's room."

"A note?"

"It looks like she went on her own."

"Why would she do that?"

"For the greater good, she said. She knew your rooms were wired. Said there's listening devices all over the house, too."

"Sounds like Elle," he muttered. Elle—risking her own safety for others. He wasn't surprised. But he couldn't let things end badly. He had to get to her.

"Where are you?"

Denton told Agent Duffield his location.

"We're five minutes behind you. Stay safe."

He cut his headlights and slowly rolled down the road, trying not to draw attention to himself. Something in the distance caught his eye. A car.

Elle's car.

He braked, threw the car in Park and stepped out. Before taking another step, he scanned the area around him. There was no movement, no sign of life. Had Elle gone into that house? He had to be cautious, to ignore the emotions that told him to rush inside and find the woman he'd fallen in love with.

He crept around the house, dodging weeds and cinder blocks and burn barrels scattered about the neglected site. No sound came from inside the house. Everything seemed quiet. Too quiet.

He'd only been ten minutes behind Elle. How far could she have gotten?

Something in the distance caught his eye. Something metallic caught a ray of moonlight. He rushed toward it and fingered the fabric. Elle's sweatshirt. The light had caught on its zipper.

His gaze traveled to the narrow path in front of him.

Elle had left him a clue.

He took off down the trail.

Elle shoved a branch out of her way. It felt like the woods were surrounding her, reaching out, desperate to take her prisoner. How far did this trail lead into the depths of the forest?

Owls hooted, insects hissed, branches snapped.

And her doubt grew.

Was it too late to turn around? To run away?

But what would happen then? Would the bomb detonate in her home?

But everyone was probably evacuated by now.

It didn't matter. These guys would find a way to make everyone suffer unless Elle decided to take their "punishment" upon herself.

Her cell phone rang, the shrill sound causing her muscles to flinch, her heart to race. She brought the phone to her ear. "Go left. We'll find you."

Her throat tightened, fear getting the best of her. "Isn't there another way? Anything else we can do?"

"Either you die or everyone else around you does. What's it going to be?"

"Me," she whispered. Her family would mourn her death, but she couldn't live with herself if she was the cause of their murders.

The forest became denser. Water from the murky ground sloshed onto her pant legs, sending a chill through her. Underbrush grabbed at her ankles.

Where were they? Were they watching her now? How would they find her?

With a bullet?

Her anxiety nearly made her double over with apprehension. Her hand scrambled to find something—anything—to help hold her up, to help propel her forward.

She paused a moment, sagged against a tree.

Just then a hand clamped over her mouth. "Ellebird. Isn't that what your grandmother called you? It's a nice name for such a pretty girl."

The man shoved her forward, allowing her to turn around. Her captor didn't wear a mask, but even in the darkness, his features came into focus.

He was…the house cleaner?

* * *

Voices drifted from the distance.

Denton veered off the trail, trying to remain hidden, to not make any sudden noises to give away his location.

Two male voices carried through the darkness.

Definitely the two men from the bank robbery. Their voices were stained in his memory. He'd bet anything these men were Thomas and Ryan Matthews.

"I'll do whatever you ask. Just leave my friends and family alone." Elle… Denton's heart twisted at the sound of her voice. He expected her to sound brittle, but instead her words carried a level, even tone.

One of the men laughed, the sound slow, methodical.

Evil.

Denton bristled. Just what were these guys planning? And how was he going to get to Elle and rescue her without hinting to her captors of his presence?

He peered around the oak tree that offered him cover, and he spotted the three of them maybe ten feet away. They stood in a small clearing in the forest, several tiki torches lit around them and affording Denton a glance at what was going on.

Sure enough, the two brothers stood there with Elle in their grasps. The tall man was Thomas Matthews, the man who'd just gotten out of prison, who was a bomb expert, and the dominant of the two. Ryan Matthews was a small man who had the look of someone working an office job. Appropriate since he was the computer genius. What a terrible mix when you put the two of these guys together.

Even worse when Elle was in the middle of them.

The nighttime seemed to gasp around him, a mix of crickets and owls and the scamper of other nocturnal creatures.

He looked down just in time to see the glimmer of a line at his feet.

A trip wire?

Had these guys wired the woods also?

The sound of Elle crying out in pain nearly had him rushing to her. He couldn't. He had to be careful, to be safe. He couldn't rescue her if he was dead.

He sidestepped the wire, his gaze roaming the forest floor for any others. They'd be nearly impossible to see. The fact that he'd seen the first one was a gift from God.

Lord, I could use Your wisdom right now. Your protection. Remind me of Your sovereignty. And keep Elle safe.

He paced forward and ducked behind another oak tree. He peered around the tree again, trying to find the right angle to take a shot. He flinched when he saw Elle's head jerked back, Ryan's hand tangled in her hair. Her eyes were wide with fear. No, not fear. Terror.

She was sacrificing herself to save everyone else in her life. Noble.

But Denton wasn't going to let that happen.

"Why are you doing this?" Elle's voice trembled now.

"You really don't know?" Thomas asked.

"I really don't know."

Thomas ran the gun down her exposed throat and paused by her heart. "Vengeance, Ellebird."

"What did I do to you?" She licked her lips, the white of her eyes still visible in the dark density of the forest. Ryan pinned Elle's arms behind her back. The man was slight, obviously more skilled in the brains department than the brawn. But hatred could make people act irrationally. It could make their adrenaline pump and give them bursts of strength and energy.

Thomas shook his head. "You? Nothing. Your father. He let our sister's killer walk. Said his hands were tied. Today, that smug little criminal is walking free while our sister lays six feet under."

"Why not go after the killer? He's the one who took your sister away. That's not my father's fault. The law is the law.

You can't change it. If my dad said there was nothing he could do—"

"Shut up!" Thomas pulled his gun back and held it in both of his hands, ready to fire. "If you let evil people walk, then you're evil yourself. There's no better revenge on someone than to hurt the people they love. Having two of his daughters killed will ruin your father. It would ruin anyone."

Denton crept forward. The situation was escalating, and he had to do something. Now. When the men were in range, he drew the gun from his holster, and aimed it right at Thomas.

Before he could pull the trigger, an explosion rocked the world behind him.

Elle screamed, her gaze darting toward the ball of fire in the distance. What was that? What had just happened?

"That could have been your boyfriend. We thought he might follow you." Before the man she still thought of as Ringleader could finish his sentence, something popped. The man clutched his shoulder, let out a curse word. Then he fell backward on the ground.

"What…?" the IT guy—Shortie—said.

He jerked Elle in front of him and put the gun to her temple. "If you know what's best for you, you won't do that again. Not if you want to see Elle live another day."

She wasn't going to live another day anyway, was she?

But that didn't mean she didn't want to.

Who had fired that bullet? Was it Denton? Had he followed her?

If so, where was he now?

The man behind her trembled. She could hear the catch to his breath, the panic in his voice. His gaze swung wildly as he searched for the source of the gunshot.

"Come out or the girl dies! I mean it. You've got to the count of three."

Ringleader moaned on the ground and continued his string of curses. But he wasn't any threat, not based on the way his face twisted with agony or the way blood stained his clothing.

"One…"

Elle's gaze darted around. She half hoped Denton would step out and half hoped that he wouldn't. As the gun shook at her temple, she realized how easy it would be for the gunman's finger to slip. Flashbacks from the bank hit her.

Lord, help us.

"No one will be able to stand against you as long as you live. For I will be with you as I was with Moses. I will not fail you or abandon you."

God was on her side. No matter how this turned out, she knew she was in her Savior's care.

And that gave her the strength to face her fears.

First, to face these madmen.

Then to face love…maybe?

Because the way her heart twisted at the thought of anything happening to Denton made it obvious that she was in love with the man.

"Two…"

A stick cracked in the distance.

What could she do? She reviewed the items she'd brought. Knife. Razors. Perfume.

She had to do something before the man shot her. She had to fight for her life. And Denton's life.

"You're not a killer," she said to Shortie. "That's your brother, you know. A judge will realize that. He's just playing you in his game of revenge here."

"What do you know? The justice system fails people all the time."

"I know your brother has always tried to control you, even when you were growing up. He made you feel inferior. He made you do his dirty work. He probably even made you take the blame." She didn't know where the thoughts came from exactly, but they made sense. She had to stall for more time.

"You don't know anything."

The gun still trembled at her temple, ratcheting up her heart rate. "You don't want to make this any worse than it already is. What happened to your sister was a terrible tragedy. I remember hearing about the case. I remember my father mourning over the outcome and wishing he could change things. But he couldn't."

"Things can't get much worse. If we're caught, we'll go to prison for life. Maybe even face execution. Either way, we're toast."

She couldn't deny his words. They were in too deep.

She eased the perfume from beneath her watch. Slowly, she adjusted it in her hands. She could do this. She could do this.

Even when her mind screamed no. When her will rebelled.

"When I say three, I'm pulling the trigger."

At once, Elle pulled her elbow back and rammed it into the man's stomach. She twirled, spraying the man's eyes with her perfume. He screamed as the spray hit his eyes. His grasp around her slipped and she jerked out of his hold.

As soon as she stepped away another pop came from the woods, hitting the man squarely on the shoulder. He hit the ground, crying out in pain.

Elle kicked the gun away from his hands.

She looked up and saw Denton step from the woods.

Tears welled in her eyes. In two strides, she was in his arms, weeping. "You shouldn't have come."

His breath was hot on her cheek. "No, you shouldn't have come. It was stupid, foolhardy—"

"I didn't know what else to do." Tears continued to wash down her face.

Denton pulled back and looked her in the eye. "And it was selfless. I wish you hadn't done it, but it did prove one thing,

Elle. It proved that you don't let fear hold you back. You would have never come here tonight if you did."

"I don't want my fears to hold me back. Especially not when it comes to…when it comes to you. I'm sorry that I doubted you."

"They did a good job with those photos, Elle. They knew how to hit you where it hurt."

"Denton, I think I'm falling in love with you." Even as the words left her mouth, she didn't feel the race of panic that she'd expected. No, she felt peace.

Denton's lips covered hers. Wrapped in his arms, she felt total. Complete. Secure. Loved.

Just then, a flurry of agents broke through the trees and surrounded them. Agent Duffield took control of the scene.

Denton pulled back and wrapped his arm around her shoulders. "Come on. Let's get you out of here, and put this nightmare behind us."

EPILOGUE

Six months later

"The paperwork is complete, the website is up, I've hired two employees and was just approved for a federal grant. Never Forgotten is up and running."

She glanced around her parents' home. Once the home of a senator. Now the home of a professor and his loving wife. Elle had never seen her mom and dad look so happy. Maybe a break from politics was what they all needed.

Elle's father had used his connections to organize a fundraiser at his home to celebrate the opening of Never Forgotten, the nonprofit she'd dreamed about for years.

Elle looked at the crowd milling around and smiled. Not only were friends and family here, but Agent Duffield had come, as well as Jack and Rachel Sergeant. And Denton, of course. Denton was always there, always supportive and always loyal.

Her eyes scanned the room. Speaking of Denton, where had he gone? Hopefully her dad hadn't stolen him away to look at the set of golf clubs he'd just purchased. Her mom and dad had decided to take up the sport together, and it was all they wanted to talk about.

Annabelle Wentworth approached, her eyes sparkling.

"Lovely fund-raiser, Elle. I'm so glad to see you doing something that makes you happy. You deserve it."

"Thank you, Annabelle."

She leaned closer, her expensive perfume nearly taking Elle's breath away. "You heard about Preston, didn't you?"

Elle shook her head.

"The engagement is off. Makes me glad the two of you didn't work out. The man has a wandering eye."

Just then, someone wrapped their arms around her from behind. "Some men don't appreciate what they've got. I more than appreciate what I've got. I treasure it."

Elle stepped to the side and grinned. Denton. He was still around, with no signs of leaving. In her heart, she knew he was the kind of man who'd be around for good.

And she wouldn't complain about that. Not one bit.

"You two! You're so adorable together. Maybe after you get this nonprofit off the ground, you should consider running for office, Elle."

Elle laughed, the chuckle starting deep within her and bellowing out long and hard.

"I'm actually hoping she'll be busy planning other things."

Elle's eyes widened. "What kind of other things?"

Denton grinned, his ever-sparkling eyes having an extra glimmer to them today. He dropped to one knee. He reached into his pocket and pulled out a tiny box. "Like maybe a wedding."

Her heart felt like it might stop as joy coursed through her.

"Elle Philips, would you do me the honor of becoming my wife?"

A crowd had gathered around them. Elle's heart raced erratically. "Yes. Yes. Absolutely, yes!"

Denton slipped a ring on her finger. A beautiful princess-cut diamond. On the band, tiny doves were engraved.

Hope.

Yes, there was always hope for the future, no matter what you'd been through.

"I love you, Mark Denton."

He stood and pulled her into his arms amid the cheers of everyone around them. "And I love you, Elle Philips."

* * * * *

Dear Reader,

Thanks for joining me on Denton and Elle's adventures in life and love. When I wrote *The Last Target* (LIS, September 2011), I knew I had to tell Denton's story, and I knew there were many other stories waiting to be told featuring the heroes working at Iron, Inc. That's when this series, The Security Experts, was born, and I was able to breathe life into some of the characters who begged me to tell their stories. Our lives aren't often filled with the same pulse-pounding danger as found in *Key Witness* (thank goodness!), but we still have the opportunity to trust God as we daily face trials and trying circumstances. Each of our lives is an adventure, and I pray that every step of the way you're able to deepen your faith and trust, just like the characters of this book.

Christy Barritt

Questions for Discussion

1. Elle has seen a lot of poor examples in her life as to what marriage should be and, as a result, has little hope that marriage is worth the risk. What kind of people have served as an example to you as to how to live your life? Were they positive or negative examples? What kind of testimony would you like your life to leave?

2. Elle thought she had Denton figured out, but she was wrong. It's easy to make quick judgments about someone without knowing the details of their life. Have you ever been wrong about someone? Has someone ever been wrong about you?

3. Elle lets her fear over disappointing others hold her back. Are there fears that hold you back? How can you move beyond your fears?

4. Denton faced the ultimate disappointment in life when his wife died of cancer. What kind of disappointments have you faced in life? How did you handle them? How did your disappointments change you? What did you learn from them to prepare you for the future?

5. Have you, like Elle, ever followed a path for your life that someone else planned for you? How did that work out? If you had it to do over again, what would you change?

6. Are there any dreams you want to pursue but haven't? Why or why not?

7. The verse that Elle constantly repeats is from Joshua, and it says, *"Wherever you set foot, you will be on land I have given you…. No one will be able to stand against you as long as you live. For I will be with you as I was with Moses. I will not fail you or abandon you."* What's a time in your life when you've been scared—either physically or emotionally? How did you get through it? What did you learn?

8. Jesus practiced the ultimate selflessness when he died on the cross. He sacrificed everything in order to give life. How does that fact change your life?

9. Elle finds comfort in the beach and her favorite pizza. Where do you go or what do you do when life feels overwhelming?

10. Elle's father learns that success comes at a price. Do you ever take time to reevaluate your priorities to make sure they're in line with God's?

11. Elle feels as if her grandmother is one of the only people who can truly see her pain. Do you have anyone like that in your life—someone who can see through your facade and into your hurts?

12. Have you ever lost someone you loved? How did you handle it? What would you tell someone else who's grieving the loss of someone in their life?

REQUEST YOUR FREE BOOKS!

2 FREE RIVETING INSPIRATIONAL NOVELS PLUS 2 FREE MYSTERY GIFTS

Love Inspired®
SUSPENSE

YES! Please send me 2 FREE Love Inspired® Suspense novels and my 2 FREE mystery gifts (gifts are worth about $10). After receiving them, if I don't wish to receive any more books, I can return the shipping statement marked "cancel." If I don't cancel, I will receive 4 brand-new novels every month and be billed just $4.49 per book in the U.S. or $4.99 per book in Canada. That's a savings of at least 22% off the cover price. It's quite a bargain! Shipping and handling is just 50¢ per book in the U.S. and 75¢ per book in Canada.* I understand that accepting the 2 free books and gifts places me under no obligation to buy anything. I can always return a shipment and cancel at any time. Even if I never buy another book, the two free books and gifts are mine to keep forever.

123/323 IDN FVWV

Name	(PLEASE PRINT)	
Address		Apt. #
City	State/Prov.	Zip/Postal Code

Signature (if under 18, a parent or guardian must sign)

Mail to the **Harlequin® Reader Service:**
IN U.S.A.: P.O. Box 1867, Buffalo, NY 14240-1867
IN CANADA: P.O. Box 609, Fort Erie, Ontario L2A 5X3

Are you a subscriber to Love Inspired Suspense and want to receive the larger-print edition? Call 1-800-873-8635 or visit www.ReaderService.com.

* Terms and prices subject to change without notice. Prices do not include applicable taxes. Sales tax applicable in N.Y. Canadian residents will be charged applicable taxes. Offer not valid in Quebec. This offer is limited to one order per household. Not valid for current subscribers to Love Inspired Suspense books. All orders subject to credit approval. Credit or debit balances in a customer's account(s) may be offset by any other outstanding balance owed by or to the customer. Please allow 4 to 6 weeks for delivery. Offer available while quantities last.

Your Privacy—The Harlequin® Reader Service is committed to protecting your privacy. Our Privacy Policy is available online at www.ReaderService.com or upon request from the Harlequin Reader Service.
We make a portion of our mailing list available to reputable third parties that offer products we believe may interest you. If you prefer that we not exchange your name with third parties, or if you wish to clarify or modify your communication preferences, please visit us at www.ReaderService.com/consumerchoice or write to us at Harlequin Reader Service Preference Service, P.O. Box 9062, Buffalo, NY 14269. Include your complete name and address.

Rookie K-9 officer Valerie Salgado saw a murder suspect leaving the scene of a crime and now needs protection.

Read on for a preview of the next book in the exciting
TEXAS K-9 UNIT *series, GUARD DUTY*
by Sharon Dunn.

"K-9 unit 349. Convenience-store robbery, corner of State and Grand. Suspects on the run."

Rookie officer Valerie Salgado hit her sirens and sped up. She reached the store, opened the back door of the patrol car and her Rottweiler, Lexi, jumped out.

Lexi found the trail, then ran hard, leading Valerie up the street, through an alley and into a residential neighborhood.

Lexi stopped suddenly in a yard that had stacks of roofing shingles piled on the walkway and a ladder propped against the roof.

The bushes in the yard shook. Valerie lifted her head just in time to see a man take off running.

Valerie clicked Lexi off the leash. Lexi leaped over the fence and bounded after the suspect.

Valerie unsnapped the holster that held her gun. She heard a scraping noise right before something crashed hard against her shoulder, knocking her to the ground.

She stumbled to her feet. Shingles. Was the second perpetrator on the roof? She hurried most of the way up the ladder using the roofline for cover.

The suspect came out from behind the chimney, aiming his gun at her. He slipped on the sharply angled roof, falling on his side and dropping the gun. The gun skittered across the shingles and fell to the ground below. This was her chance.

Valerie scrambled up the ladder. "Put your hands up."

The man dashed toward her. He intended to push the ladder away from the roof!

The suspect's feet seemed to be pulled out from under him, and he slammed facedown on the roof. As the suspect scrambled to his feet, she saw the silhouette of a second man, tall and broad through the shoulders.

The second man landed a blow to the suspect's face, knocking him on his back.

Her rescuer stepped out of the shadows. "Officer Salgado, why don't you wait at the bottom? I'll stay up here and make sure this guy doesn't get any ideas."

She had no idea who this man was or where he had come from, but everything about him said law enforcement and he knew her name. "Who are you?"

Will Valerie's rescuer turn her life upside down?
Pick up GUARD DUTY by Sharon Dunn,
available March 2013 from Love Inspired Suspense.

Love Inspired ®
SUSPENSE

RIVETING INSPIRATIONAL ROMANCE

FRAMED!

With a body left at the doorstep of his Wyoming ranch, single dad Wyatt Monroe gets arrested for murder, and Wyatt's only hope is a blue-eyed, blonde female bodyguard. It'll take more than skill for work-obsessed Jackie Blain to save her client. After her fiancé dumped her for another woman, she has no intentions of letting anyone get that close again even though she longs for a family to call her own. But with the lives of a handsome cowboy and a charming daughter in her hands, she's faced with her toughest assignment ever—saving the cowboy and guarding her heart.

PROTECTION SPECIALISTS

Guarding the innocent

THE COWBOY TARGET

by

TERRI REED

**Available in March
wherever books are sold.**

www.LoveInspiredBooks.com

LIS44529